Dead in the Water

AJ BASINSKI

I dedicate this book to my wife, Betsy, without whom it could not have been written.

"Only the hand that erases can write the true thing."

Meister Eckhart
13th c. German mystic

1

"Lieutenant Morales, Lieutenant Morales, please wake up, sir. Hurry. We need your help right away. Lieutenant Morales, please sir".

I rolled over in bed and pulled the alarm clock closer to my face so that I could read it better. The clock's dial glowed 5:00 in a sickening green color. Was that a.m. or p.m.? I really had no idea. It seemed like I had a hard time remembering things lately. In fact, I wasn't even too sure how I had ended up back in my own cabin. Or at least I thought it was my own cabin.

"Lieutenant Morales, please answer me if you are in there. We need your help right away. We think there may have been a murder on board the ship." The voice sounded to me like a roar, even through the thick cabin door.

After a few seconds, I got my bearings and was finally able to recognize the voice as belonging to one of the new security guards I had recently hired to replace two guards who had been fired for drug smuggling shortly before I was hired as head of security on board the Mardi Gras.

"Roman, Roman, something or other," I mumbled as I rolled over onto my back, as I finally remembered the name of the man whose voice I heard outside my stateroom door. "What the hell does he want at this time of the morning," I wondered. "Goddamn him, just when I was starting to fall asleep after being awake all night."

The pounding on my door continued but all I wanted was to be left alone. I had a throbbing, migraine headache, and I felt like I might throw up. I did recall that the Captain's welcoming party the night before had gone on for a lot longer than usual and I had drunk way too much tequila. I did not particularly like tequila, but there was a certain young woman at the party, who I was drinking with and she loved tequila. Lots of it. I could barely keep up with her as we downed tequila sunrises together at dinner and later at the bar in the ship's lounge. Truth be told, I hadn't had a drink in over a year since I left LA. Little wonder I felt so lousy now.

"What was her name? I'm not sure that she even told me." I thought that she was Asian----

Chinese, or Vietnamese or maybe, Korean, but I wasn't even sure about that. But I was certain that she was quite beautiful. She wore her long black hair down to her waist and her eyelashes seemed almost as long. She had on a black, silk, split leg dress that was slit to her hip and showed off her surprisingly long brown legs. I thought she looked incredibly sexy. "I must look her up this morning."

"Get me some coffee. Black, no sugar," I yelled as I started to climb out of the narrow single bed. "I'll be right out." I climbed slowly out of bed and stood up and immediately I realized that the ship was not moving. Usually, when the ship is moving, I feel a little unsteady when I first get out of bed or stand up from a chair. When I was being interviewed for the job as head of security aboard the Mardi Gras, I had told the interviewer that I had lived my whole life in California and had never been on a ship before. He assured me, "Don't worry; you'll get your sea legs in no time." He was wrong. It had been six months and I still seemed to feel woozy half the time.

Once out of bed, I walked over to the far side of the cabin and looked out the small porthole. The ship was enveloped in a thick, black fog. I couldn't tell where the water ended and the sky began, it was so thick. We must be stopped in the middle of the Gulf of Mexico. I hoped it was only the fog and not some mechanical problem that had caused the ship to be dead in the water.

There had been a rash of mechanical problems recently on all of the Mariner cruise ships. A few months before I came on board, there had been a suspicious fire in the engine room of the Mardi Gras, which had required the evacuation of the ship. Passengers aboard all four of the Mariner ships also had gotten violently ill from the norovirus. The cruise line's public relations department had issued press releases claiming that all of these intestinal problems were caused by the passengers themselves. But, because of these problems, the cruise line had become fodder for the late night, television talk show hosts almost every night. Bookings were definitely down as a result and Mariner had recently filed for bankruptcy.

I had been chief of security on the Mardi Gras for almost six months. I had found life aboard the Mardi Gras to be quite pleasant. Since I had come on board, I and my deputy, and our crew of eight security guards had investigated several robberies and assaults on board the ship. Most of these were of a petty nature. I made sure that security aboard the ship was quite tight because it is well known that some passengers on cruise ships are affluent and travel with a considerable amount of cash and jewelry. For that reason, a variety of petty criminals and a few well-trained thieves stalk the cruise ships to prey on those passengers. But murder? I quickly dismissed the thought that there had been a murder on board my ship. Not that I wasn't familiar with murder. I had seen plenty of murders while working homicide out of the Ramparts Division west of downtown Los Angeles, where there were frequent homicides in that most-densely populated part of the city.

But, undoubtedly, I said to myself, this supposed murder on board the ship, will turn out to be nothing but a false alarm. It was early March and there were hundreds of college kids aboard the ship for spring break, many of whom got quite drunk on the mai tais and other drinks that freely flowed aboard the ship. I thought that this "murder" may just be one of those college pranks that those kids loved to play on the crew just for the hell of it.

I convinced myself that Roman had failed to examine all of the facts. The facts do not lie, I said to myself. For me, Roman was just a little too excitable and I may have to reconsider his hiring, Little did I know how wrong I would turn out to be.

"I hear you, you idiot. I hear you. Now just keep quiet. You'll wake up the whole damn ship." The last thing that I wanted to happen was to have Roman create a panic among the passengers on the ship with these cries of "murder." Some of the passengers who were awake were probably already wondering why the ship was stopped in the middle of the Gulf of Mexico. Now, if they heard about a murder on the ship---well, who knows what might happen.

Every week, the Mardi Gras sailed between Miami and Cozumel, Mexico, with a short day stop in Key West, Florida. The four and five day cruises ran between early January and early May. At one time, the Mardi Gras had been a state of the art cruise ship, but now it had seen better days. Several times during the last year or so, it had stopped dead in the water due to mechanical problems.

The Mardi Gras generally had almost 2000 passengers on board as well as a crew of at least

1000. The logistics of providing food for those 3000 people were astounding. The logistics of interviewing those same 3000 people about a potential murder or disappearance were even more frightening to me.

Yet each of those 3000 people was a potential witness who might add something to the puzzle if indeed there was a murder. On the other hand, we were still a day's sail away from Miami. The last thing we needed was to stir up mass hysteria among the passengers and crew if they thought a murderer was loose among them.

"I'll be right out, goddamn it. And quiet down, for God's sake," I yelled through the door.

The last thing I did after getting dressed and before leaving my cabin was to put on my St. Michael medal which I wore on a silver chain around my neck. I never went anywhere without it. St. Michael was the patron saint of police officers and I believed he had saved my life more than once. I had been an altar boy when I was a kid and even thought about becoming a priest. My mother would have loved it if I had been ordained a priest, but I realized when I was a teenager that I was not cut out for the religious life. But I still believed and tried to get to Mass as often as I could. When I was still on the LAPD, some of the other cops would call me "St. Mario" because I went to Mass so often. I sort of liked the nickname.

"So, where is this so-called murder," I said as I stepped out of my stateroom into the narrow hall. I was surprised to see not only Roman, but also Sergeant Virginia Boudreaux, my deputy and, most surprisingly, Captain Antonio Vivaldi, the captain of the Mardi Gras. The Captain was wearing his immaculate dress white uniform, which looked as though it had just come back from the dry cleaners. I had been told that some crew members sometimes joked about Vivaldi because his name was the same as the famed Italian composer and they had heard the Captain playing Vivaldi's music in his cabin long into the night. I myself preferred Herbie Hancock's jazz albums.

"This must be serious to get you out of bed this early, Tony" I joked to the Captain. But Vivaldi did not laugh and said nothing in response.

"Lieutenant, I think you should take this matter seriously," said Sergeant Boudreaux. "We believe a woman may have been murdered on her honeymoon."

"So, you believe a woman has been murdered," I said. "And on her honeymoon, no less. Well, tell me, where is the body?"

"Well, sir, there is no body," piped up Roman.

"No body, but a murder has been committed. Very interesting. This is an impossibility. Why are you wasting my time? Are you sure this is not just one of those spring break pranks?" I was still irritated at being awakened so early in the morning and I was almost ready to turn back and return to my cabin to sleep off this powerful hangover that was gripping me.

"It is very complex" said Captain Vivaldi.

"Murder is always complex, Tony. But you must have a body." I continued, "And who is this woman who has been murdered."

Captain Vivaldi again responded, "Her name is Linda Weigand. She is on the cruise ship with her new husband, Robert. It was her husband who called to report that she was missing and that he suspected she may have been murdered."

Suddenly, this disappearance took on a totally new flavor. Maybe this was something more than just a fraternity brothers' prank.

"I will want to speak to Mr. Weigand myself, of course, but what did he tell you had happened to his new bride?"

This time Sergeant Boudreaux answered, "I was the one who took the call since you and Captain Vivaldi were both asleep. Mr. Weigand said he had last seen his wife around midnight or so in the ship's casino. He said he and his wife had been there for a couple of hours. He says that he had lost several hundred dollars playing blackjack. He claims he told his wife that he was very tired and that he wanted to go back to their cabin to sleep. Mrs. Weigand told him that she wanted to stay a little longer at the casino and asked Mr. Weigand for some money to play blackjack. He says he gave her two one- hundred dollar bills, kissed her goodbye and left her at one of the blackjack tables. As he was leaving the casino, he saw his boss, Joe Hugo, coming into the casino. He says that he saw Hugo sit down next to Linda at the blackjack table. That was the last time he saw her."

"Who is this Hugo guy? You say he was Weigand's boss? I thought you said that this was the couple's honeymoon. What was he doing on the ship? Who goes on a honeymoon with their boss?"

Captain Vivaldi answered, "Hugo is a wealthy automobile dealer in the Miami area. According to Forbes he is one of the wealthiest car dealers in the United States. I am told that he has about a dozen different dealerships throughout South Florida, mostly selling Hondas. You probably have seen his commercials on television. Both of the Weigands worked for him. The Weigands had just been married a few weeks before. The cruise was a wedding gift for the two of them from Hugo."

I was puzzled as to why the Captain seemed to know so much about the Weigands and Hugo, but decided not to pursue it for now. We had a more pressing thing to consider: where was Linda Weigand and why had she disappeared.

I asked the group, "Has anyone talked to Hugo? It sounds like he may have been the last person to have seen her." No one responded to my question and I assumed no one had talked to Hugo. "I will want to talk to him shortly," I said. My assumption would turn out to be wrong as I would later find out that Sergeant Boudreaux had already spoken to him.

I continued: "Sounds like she may be missing. So why does Weigand think his wife has been murdered?"

Sergeant Boudreaux answered very quickly, "Weigand told me that after he left the ship's casino, he went back to his suite and crashed on the bed and fell asleep right away. This was a little after midnight, he thought. About two o'clock he said he heard a loud noise from the suite next door but he said that despite the noise he was able to fall asleep again. When he woke up a couple of hours later, he was very surprised to see that Mrs.Weigand was not in bed with him or anywhere else in the room. He knew that the casino had closed by then so he says he panicked. First thing he did was to call her cell phone. He tried multiple times, but got no answer. Weigand says he left a couple of messages on her phone, but he never heard back from her. Weigand claims that his wife always carries her cell and always returns messages right away. He says he was frightened that something might have happened to her and decided to search the ship looking for her. He told me that he walked around the ship two, maybe three times; he wasn't sure which because he was in such a daze. When he didn't find her, he called the security office. Because I was on the night watch when the call came in, I was the one who spoke to him. I then woke up the Captain and contacted the others before coming to your cabin just now."

I was quite upset that Boudreaux had awakened the Captain and the others before coming to me. Boudreaux seemed more and more like my ex-wife. But that's a whole other story. For now though, I decided to brush it off as just another example of Boudreaux' over -eagerness.

"So, based on what he told you all we know for sure is that she is missing," I said. "You still haven't answered my question, 'Why does Weigand think she was murdered?'"

"You'll have to ask him that yourself," said

Boudreaux. "Weigand broke down and started crying during my discussion with him and we never got that far. All he said was 'She must be dead or I would have heard from her by now.' Because he seemed so distraught, I put him in touch with Doc Phillips and Doc gave him a tranquilizer to try and calm him down."

"Where is Weigand now?" I asked.

This time Captain Vivaldi answered, "He's in my quarters."

Strange, I thought. I'll need to find out more about why the Captain is giving Weigand this special treatment.

"All right," I began, "let's fan out and search the ship from top to bottom. If she is still on this ship, we will find her, I'm sure. I want each of you to take at least two decks to search. Divide them up as you see fit. Check everything, including the lifeboats and anything else that may be covered or any place where she might be hidden. I will search the Lido deck myself. Let's hope we will be able to find her. Use your discretion if you see one of the passengers during your search. If they ask why you are walking the ship, just say it's routine, that we do it every morning. Got that? Make sure that you check the water as well. I know it will be difficult to see much because of the fog, but if she fell or jumped overboard, she might still be near the ship since we are stopped in the water for now. After we are done with our search, I will look at the surveillance tapes of the water surrounding the ship and the ship's public spaces."

Before our little group split up, I said, "Oh,

and by the way, what does Linda Weigand look like? I guess that it would be helpful if we knew what she looked like. Anyone have a picture?"

Captain Vivaldi was the one who responded this time, "I have a picture taken at her recent wedding. She is tall with long red hair. She is a very pretty young woman, as you can see. I pray nothing has happened to her."

Vivaldi handed me the small, wallet-sized photograph and I passed it around to the others. She was indeed very pretty. Standing next to her in the photograph was apparently her husband, Robert. He also was tall and very good looking with a wide, toothy grin.

Once again what surprised me most was how much the Captain seemed to know about the Weigands. And how did he come into possession of her wedding photograph? For now though, I decided to let it go. It was more important that we find this woman first and ask these types of questions later.

"All right, let's spread out and begin the search. Wake up the other security guards if you need more help in the search. Remember to take your time and be thorough. There are lots of nooks and crannies on this ship. Let's say that we meet back in my office in an hour to report on what you have discovered. If you do happen to find her before then, call me immediately on my cell phone. All right, good luck and see you in an hour."

As we began to separate and head off in different directions, I called after the Captain, "Tony, what the hell happened to the ship? Why are we dead in the water?"

Vivaldi turned and snapped, "The fog, the fog, of course. I stopped the ship last night when the fog rolled in. Do you think I am going to run the ship aground like that crazy guy in Italy who wrecked the Costa ship and killed all those people when he was showing off to his girlfriend?" The captain then stomped off down the long, narrow corridor.

2

Three weeks before the disappearance of Linda Weigand while on board the Mardi Gras, Bud Gorley was sitting at his large, mahogany desk in his Miami law office. He was working on revisions to a brief that was due the next day in the Eleventh Circuit Court of Appeals. Gorley was writing the brief, seeking the affirmance of a jury award of six million dollars in favor of his client, a forty-three year old paraplegic who had been injured in a crash with a tractor trailer on the Tamiami Trail. He thought that the brief still needed quite a lot of work before it was ready for filing. One of his young associates had initially drafted the brief and Gorley was now sorry he had given the assignment to him. As he was marking up the brief with his revisions and suggestions, Gorley's legal assistant, Avery, entered his office.

"Mr. Gorley," she said, "I am very sorry to interrupt you like this, but there is a man named Yao Lin on the telephone. He says he needs to speak to you immediately. He claims it is a matter of great importance."

Gorley looked up at Avery and thought for a moment about whether he recognized the name. The name certainly did not sound familiar to him.

"Tell him I'm busy and I will get back to him tomorrow," Gorley said rather abruptly. "I really do have to finish this brief."

"I already told him that, sir, but he insisted that he needed to talk to you right away. He actually said that it is a matter of life and death."

"Avery, how many times have we heard that before?" Gorley replied.

"I know, sir. It always seems like everyone needs you immediately and has a life and death crisis."

"Oh, all right, I'll take the call," Gorley said finally.

As Avery left the office and closed the door behind her, Gorley pushed the flashing light on his desk telephone and said, "This is Bud Gorley, how may I help you?"

"Mr. Gorley, my name is Yao Lin," the voice at the other end began. "I am the assistant Chinese trade ambassador to the United States. I am very sorry to bother you, Mr. Gorley; I know that you are a very busy man."

Suddenly, this call sounded a lot more interesting to Gorley. The assistant Chinese trade ambassador to the United States, Gorley thought to himself, why would he be calling me?

Without missing a beat, Gorley said, "I am never too busy to speak to a potential client, which is what I hope you will be."

"But of course, Mr. Gorley, that is why I am calling you. My country is in need of your legal services and I would like to speak to you about a matter of great importance to my country. You come very highly recommended and we believe that you have certain capabilities that we are looking for."

"I'm quite flattered," said Gorley, knowing full well that this was probably all BS, but he loved to hear it, regardless. "What kind of matter are you talking about?" Gorley asked.

"I prefer not to speak of it on the telephone, Mr. Gorley, because of the sensitivity of the matter. Would it be possible to speak with you in person? Say, tomorrow morning."

"Hold one second, "Gorley said as he covered the phone's mouthpiece with his hand.

"What do I have on tap tomorrow?" he asked Avery over the intercom.

"Nothing that can't wait. Except of course the appeals brief you are working on."

"Mr. Yao, yes, tomorrow will work out just fine," said Gorley as he returned to the call. "How is ten o'clock?"

"Very good, Mr. Gorley. That should work quite well for me as well. We will see you then. Good bye."

"Avery" he said into the intercom, "mark my calendar or a meeting with Mr. Yao Lin at ten o'clock tomorrow morning, while I finish rewriting this brief. And call Rodney and tell him that I want to see him later tonight. I want to talk to him about this brief. He really needs to learn how to write a better brief. This is garbage as it is now. We'll never get the Court to affirm the judgment in our favor the way it is written now. It is going to take me half the night to fix it."

Later that evening, after he had finished revising the brief to his satisfaction, Gorley called in his associate, Rodney Kenny, and thoroughly reamed him out for his shoddy work on the brief. Gorley was satisfied he had made his point to the young associate when, after Rodney had left, Gorley saw that the back of the black leather chair where the associate had been sitting was covered in sweat. Rodney had sweated all the way through his Brooks Brothers shirt and suit.

Gorley then went on line to see if he could find out any information on this Yao Lin who was so anxious to see him. He Googled Yao and several short articles about him turned up. It seemed that Mr. Yao was not only the assistant Chinese trade representative to the United States, but also the CEO of a Chinese company named Shanghai Blue. Yet, when he typed in the term "Shanghai Blue" in Google, nothing else showed up. Rather strange, thought Gorley.

Gorley, like most of us, knew that the Chinese hold a large chunk of the debt of the United States. For years they have bought United States Treasury notes and other U.S. government securities to the tune of well over $1 trillion. Gorley's search also turned up some lesser-known information concerning the Chinese investment in the United States. He located several articles that discussed the buying spree that the Chinese have been going on in the United States. Gorley learned that the Chinese have been buying as many businesses as they can in the United States, particularly in the energy and transportation industries. A few years ago the Federal government had tried to curtail some of those acquisitions by the Chinese. But now, according to some newspaper accounts that Gorley read, it appeared that all the restrictions were off and the Chinese were going on another buying binge. This time they were buying real estate, particularly in New York City.

Not everyone was happy with all of these acquisitions by the Chinese. Gorley read that recently there had been several protests at the Chinese embassy in Washington. The protesters were objecting to China's increasing influence over the United States financial and real estate markets. The protests were nothing too serious for the most part, but Gorley read that there was a firebomb that had been thrown at the Chinese consulate in San Francisco. The firebomb badly damaged the large mahogany doors of the consulate, but fortunately no one was hurt. The police speculated that right-wing extremists were behind the bombing, but no person or group had taken responsibility for the bombing.

Gorley wondered why the Chinese were now coming to him because he was neither a corporate nor real estate lawyer. Litigation, civil or criminal, was his expertise. And he thought of himself as the best trial lawyer in South Florida, if not all of Florida.

3

After I had left the Captain and the others on the search team, I began my search of the Lido deck. I circled around the deck some four times, looking for the elusive Linda Weigand, whether dead or alive. I was wearing what I like to call my Truman outfit: white linen pants and a flowered, Hawaiian shirt that I could leave untucked. It was similar to the shirts that I saw President Harry Truman wearing in photographs when he stayed during the winter months at the Little White House in Key West in the late nineteen forties and early fifties.

The shirts had the advantage of not only disguising the extra 20 pounds I had picked up since joining the crew of the Mardi Gras, but also covering my 9mm Walther P99 which I wore in a leather holster attached to my belt just as I had done when I was still with the LAPD. The Walther was not standard issue, but I just liked the feel of it. It weighed a little less than a pound and a half. Fully loaded with 15 rounds in the magazine, it had an effective range of over 60 yards and it might just give me the extra firepower if I needed it when I came up against the bad guys. Although I had never used it, I had also worn a Colt .22 in an ankle holster as a "throwaway," just in case I needed it.

Wearing the Truman shirts when I made my rounds every morning, I thought that I looked just like another vacationer on the ship, out for a stroll along the ship's decks. I always like to make my rounds in person even though there are hundreds of surveillance cameras on the ship that beam pictures of almost every nook and cranny of the ship back to the monitors in my security office. Sometimes I would get so bored watching the monitors there that I thought I was watching endless re-runs of the seventies "Love Boat" television series. But this morning I was not out for a stroll nor to banish boredom, I knew I was on a potentially life and death search.

As I toured the Lido deck this morning, I made sure to check under the covers of the life boats that hung over the sides of the ship to see if she might be hiding there or if her body had been hidden there. I also looked closely in the area around the pool and in the pool itself. I climbed up to the performance stage that sat above the rest of the deck and checked behind the large speakers that sat there. In a few hours, the pool and the stage would be filled with crewmembers and passengers enjoying themselves--laughing, dancing and singing, but for now it was eerily quiet. I did not find Linda Weigand.

I suspected that the others would not find her either. When the search team assembled again in my office about an hour later as I had requested, they confirmed that none of them had found Mrs. Weigand lurking in the corridors or the laundry room or anywhere else on board the ship.

"Where do we go from here?" asked Captain Vivaldi.

"Three things," I replied. "First, I will continue the investigation. I will need to interview Weigand and Hugo, of course. And probably the bartender in the casino where she was playing when her husband says he last saw her. Second, I will want to review the surveillance tapes from the security cameras to see if there is anything on those tapes that might help explain her disappearance. Lastly, once I finish my initial investigation, I will contact the FBI and the Dade County police to fill them in on what is going on here so that they are aware of the situation when we return to Miami."

"No need to do that," said Sergeant Boudreaux.

"Why not?" I said.

"Because I have already called both agencies. I called them both first thing this morning after my interview with Robert Weigand."

"And who authorized you to do that?" I said as casually as I could even though I was very upset at what I perceived as a breach of protocol.

"It is not a question of authorization. It's a question of good police work and good teamwork. Who knows when we might need their help," Boudreaux answered.

"And what if we find out that Linda Weigand has not been murdered or isn't even missing. Maybe, just maybe, she is shacking up with some other guy on the ship. You know, stuff like that happens all the time. People sometimes get all liquored up on board the ship and end up in bed with the nearest person. How foolish will we look then if that is the case and Mrs.Weigand turns up back in her stateroom at noon after a night of rolling in the hay with another man?"

I had made it clear to Sergeant Boudreaux

on several occasions that it is strictly my decision as to when to bring in the other authorities for their help and how I believed investigations should be conducted. There was nothing worse in my mind than someone who did not go through the proper channels or did not follow the standard investigative protocols. And in the chain of command, I was her boss and she should have gone through me rather than going over my head. I could never forget how my ex-wife had gone to my division commander when I was having my problems dealing with the fallout from the bungled Hinchley case. I wondered if some of my anger towards her had spilled over to my relationship with Boudreaux. She and I had come from very different backgrounds and that also may have colored my initial judgment of her.

4

I was born and raised in Salinas, California. My father, Emanuel, worked in the fields picking lettuce, sometimes having to pick three thousand heads a day just to make a living for our family. He had worked with Cesar Chavez, who had led the migrant farm workers movement in the 1960s and 1970s. My father considered Chavez to be somewhat of a saint and his picture was prominently displayed in our house alongside those of John F. Kennedy and of course, Jesus Christ, as the Good Shepherd.

My mother, in addition to raising her six children, worked as a cleaning lady for Father McCahey at the Church of the Holy Innocents, where she attended daily Mass. Maybe that's where I got some of my piety. Both our parents taught my sisters and me to always work hard and follow the rules.

I had spent almost 25 years on the LAPD, mostly working homicide, before I decided to pull the pin and retire. Following the rules was deeply ingrained in me from that experience and in my approach to solving crimes, particularly a potential homicide like this one.

I knew that Boudreaux came from a very different background. I had learned that her father, who had run a small Cajun restaurant in New Orleans, died when she was only three years old. Her mother then took her and her brother to New York City where she raised them as a single mom. After

Boudreaux graduated from high school, she got a job as a secretary in the office of the New York City police commissioner. She found out she liked police work and the commissioner encouraged her to apply to the police academy. She did apply and was accepted. I had heard that she had graduated first in her class at the academy.

Before moving to Florida about a year ago, Boudreaux had spent 8 years as an undercover cop with the NYPD at a precinct near Harlem, mostly doing drug busts. It was dangerous work, I knew, that had kept her out all hours of the day and night on the streets, hustling drugs that would support a prosecution and take at least some of the dope off the streets. I knew that undercover cops were a different breed; they operated by their own rules. Think Serpico. To me that represented chaos.

The undercover work was definitely stressful on Boudreaux's marriage. After five years of marriage to another cop, who worked a regular 9 to 5 job at a desk job in a precinct on the Upper East Side, she and her husband decided to go their separate ways. Given my own problems with my ex-wife, maybe we weren't so different after all.

I also felt that she resented me since I got the job as head of security instead of her. Boudreaux had been hired as deputy head of security about six months before I was hired. When the prior head of security was fired, she naturally assumed that she would get the job. When I was hired instead, I could tell that clearly created some tension between us. Occasionally, those tensions had boiled over into our work relationship.

Just recently, Boudreaux and I had clashed over the handling of the investigation of a claim by two college girls that they had been raped by one of the ship's stewards. I had assigned her to conduct the interrogation of the steward that the two girls had identified as the rapist. After a five hour interrogation by Boudreaux, the steward confessed. When I viewed the tape of the interrogation, I realized that Boudreaux had been putting words in the mouth of the steward by browbeating and threatening him. The steward, a Filipino, barely spoke English and it was unclear to me that he even understood what he was confessing to. To me it seemed like Boudreaux was more interested in obtaining a confession than in finding out the truth of what had really happened and I had told her that. She didn't speak to me for two days afterwards. That was just like what my ex-wife would do.

I later questioned the steward myself in Spanish and he denied everything and said it could not have been him who raped the two girls. Based on what he told me I discovered that the steward had been in the ship's infirmary the entire night of the alleged rape, violently ill from a stomach virus. Doc Phillips, the ship's doctor, was able to confirm this to me since he had spent the whole night with the steward, treating him.

Doc Phillips was a man I knew I could trust. He was an imposing man, well over six feet tall, with a shock of curly gray hair. You couldn't tell by looking at him, but he was well over seventy years old and had survived two heart attacks. His wife, Jane, had died unexpectedly two years ago after 45 years of marriage. With her gone, he felt he could no longer stay in their home in Minneapolis and decided to take a job as ship's doctor aboard the Mardi Gras.

As I learned afterwards from my own questioning of the crew, the steward's cousin, who closely resembled the steward, had bragged to a number of crew members that he had sex with two girls in one night on board the ship. When I questioned him, he denied raping the girls, claiming they had lured him into their room when he came to their room to deliver extra towels and that the sex was entirely consensual. Despite his claim, I had no choice but to have him placed in shackles and put in the ship's brig. Later, I turned him over to the Miami/Dade police when we landed in Miami.

I had recently learned that the two girls and their parents had sued the Mariner cruise line for negligence in hiring the crew member and in allowing the rape to occur aboard the ship. The cruise line's lawyer had told me that I would likely be deposed as a witness in that case. That was nothing new for me; I had often testified in court in criminal cases, but it concerned me, nonetheless, because the attorney for the parents and the two girls was "Bud" Gorley. Just before the present cruise began, I was served with a subpoena for a deposition in Miami at Gorley's offices a week after the ship returned to port.

5

I knew Gorley by his reputation and his constant barrage of publicity. It sometimes seemed like Bud Gorley was all over the television news and talk shows almost every day. If there was a high-profile case in South Florida, he undoubtedly would be there on the news with the grieving widow of a man shot by the police or the defiant defendant who denied stabbing his ex-wife to death thirty-eight times. If there was a case where he was not representing a party, he could be found on CNN with Anderson Cooper, giving his opinion of the merits of the latest high profile murder case. It all began for him with the OJ Simpson case when he was asked by a local Miami station to provide commentary on the eight month long trial. He did such a good job, he was called back again and again. Eventually, he landed a position with Court TV. The publicity generated by his appearances on that network gave his legal practice an incredible boost. From a down and out lawyer who was scrambling for business when he came out of law school, he had developed into one of the most recognizable lawyers in America.

And when Gorley wasn't on the news or Court TV, his commercials would be running endlessly during the daytime quiz shows and talk shows on every local channel and cable station in South Florida. In those ads, Gorley would stand next to his cream-colored Rolls Royce (or sometimes, his powder blue Porsche) in front of his huge Tudor mansion and tell the audience of potential litigants:

"I'm Bud Gorley and if you were injured on the job or in a car accident, call me first. I'll get you the money you deserve and it won't cost you a cent unless I get money for you." He would then point to his automobile and the Tudor mansion behind him, suggesting to the gullible that they too could have that lifestyle if they just hired him to represent them. Like the Budweiser beer commercials, he always ended his commercials with the catch-phrase, "I'm Bud Gorley and 'This Bud's for *You!*'" Anheuser-Busch, the maker of Budweiser, wasn't particularly happy with Gorley's use of its iconic phrase and had sued Gorley to force him to stop using it. Gorley refused and the case remained pending.

6

As Yao Lin had promised in their phone conversation the day before, he arrived at Gorley's office at precisely 10:00 o'clock the following morning. He came with two large Chinese men, both of whom were carrying guns as Gorley could plainly see from the bulges under their arms. Gorley had often seen those bulges on some of his own criminal clients. Although Yao did not introduce the two men, he did introduce the beautiful, young lady who was also with him. He said that she was his associate, Sun Li. She was dressed exquisitely, all in black, and wore very large, round sunglasses. Gorley thought she gave him a knowing smile when Yao had finished the introduction. She was a real looker, thought Gorley, who had an eye for the ladies.

Yao, himself, was not very impressive in his appearance. He stood about five foot two inches tall and wore thick horn-rimmed glasses. Gorley thought he looked a lot like one of those North Korean dictators. But Gorley did notice that Yao was wearing a custom-made, silk suit, from Hong Kong, Gorley surmised.

Gorley ushered the three men and Sun Li into his main conference room, just outside his office. The conference room walls were covered with his college and law school diplomas, bar association awards, all bearing his full name, "R. Stirling Gorley IV." "Bud" was just a nickname his mother had given him when he was a baby back in Georgia where he grew up on the family's peanut farm, not far from the farm of former President Jimmy Carter. The nickname had just stuck all these years. Even some judges occasionally called him "Bud" in the courtroom, which would drive opposing counsel crazy because they felt like they were being railroaded by the judge.

The conference room was dominated by a large, full-length portrait of Gorley himself that hung on one wall. Gorley had commissioned the portrait from a local artist for his 50th birthday. It looked rather like something one might see in an English country house. He thought he looked quite dapper in his own navy, Saville Row bespoke suit and even bluer Countess Mara necktie that his wife had given him for Christmas one year. The color of the tie perfectly matched his very blue eyes.

"May I offer you some coffee or if you prefer some tea?" asked Gorley. "I have some Earl Grey that I brought back from London a few months ago. I picked it up at Harrods's department store. It is their house blend and it is really quite good. I'm told that the Queen has it every morning for breakfast. My assistant, Avery, can bring it right in for us."

"That is not necessary, Mr. Gorley. I prefer something, how shall I say it, maybe a little stronger. Do you have any scotch?" asked Yao. "Preferably, Johnnie Walker Blue."

"As it happens, I do," Gorley said as he walked over to the book case on the side wall next to his diploma from law school. He pushed a panel of the large bookcase and a lazy Susan twirled around, producing several bottles of top shelf scotch, vodka, and bourbon, as well as a half dozen or so cocktail glasses and a gold-colored ice bucket.

"On the rocks or neat?" Gorley asked. Here was a man who appreciated the very best Scotch, just like himself, Gorley thought. We will undoubtedly work well together.

"Neat."

"And how about the young lady and the other gentlemen, what can I get for them?"

"They don't drink," said Yao.

Gorley noticed that Sun Li seemed somewhat disappointed and he said to her, "Would you like a soft drink or water?"

She nodded yes and Gorley poured water from a Waterford pitcher into a glass tumbler and handed it to her. She seemed quite pleased, thought Gorley.

Yao downed the Johnnie Walker that Gorley had placed in front of him on the conference table. Yao then silently indicated to Gorley with wave of his hands that he would like another scotch. Gorley quickly complied, taking the opportunity to pour a scotch for both Yao and himself.

After Yao had drunk the second Scotch, Yao began, "Mr. Gorley,"

"Please, call me Bud, everybody else does."

Yao began again, "Mr. Gorley, we need your assistance in a matter of great importance to the people of China."

"I am flattered that you have come to me with your problem. How can I help you?" replied Gorley.

"You are familiar with the Mariner Cruise

Line?" asked Yao in perfect, unaccented English. Gorley learned later that Yao had spent seven years in the United States and had graduated first in his class at the Harvard Business School some twenty years earlier.

"Yes, of course," responded Gorley.

"I understand you have had some involvement with litigation against the Mariner Cruise Line."

Gorley replied, "Why yes, I have a suit pending against Mariner for negligence in connection with a rape of two young girls on board one of its ships. Nasty business. One of the crew members raped these two girls while they were on break from college. I know the father of one of the girls and he came to me with the case. The Mardi Gras, I believe was the ship involved. I am scheduled to begin taking depositions in the case very soon. One of the first people I am deposing is the chief of security aboard the Mardi Gras. I think his name is Morales, yes, Mario Morales."

"Just so," said Yao.

The girls and the girls' parents had filed a multi-million dollar lawsuit against the cruise line for its alleged negligence in hiring the rapist and in not taking proper precautions to prevent the rapes from occurring on board the ship. It was just the kind of case that Gorley loved. Gorley was counting on a large fee from that case and was hoping he could negotiate an early settlement. But the cruise line and its insurer were playing hard ball and it did not look like that case would soon settle. If the cruise line or its insurer did not settle, they ran the risk of being "gored" by Gorley, a favorite phrase among the members of the insurance defense bar in Miami. Some of those lawyers actually took pride in telling others that they had been "gored" because it meant that those lawyers were in the big leagues where they were up against the best. And make no mistake about it; Gorley was among the best when it came to trying cases, criminal or civil.

Gorley handed a third glass of neat Johnnie Walker to Yao and said, "What can I do for you?"

"You are aware," continued Yao, "that Mariner is in bankruptcy, of course."

"Yes," Gorley responded. Gorley was quite aware of the pending bankruptcy and that was another reason for his urgency in settling the rape case on behalf of the two women and their families. Gorley knew that if the case did not settle soon, he ran the risk of losing everything if the bankruptcy court decided to wipe out all pre-existing debts and obligations, including personal injury actions such as he had brought against Mariner on behalf of the girls and their parents.

Yao continued, "We also understand that you are familiar with a man named Joe Hugo, is that correct?"

"Yes, I know Hugo; we belong to the same yacht club." Gorley was a little surprised at how much Yao seemed to know about his law practice and now even his acquaintances, like Hugo. Obviously, Gorley thought, this man has done his homework.

Gorley knew Joe Hugo only in passing. But, he knew that Joe Hugo was well known for his loud and boisterous television commercials that ran incessantly on the local network and cable stations. Hugo would come on the screen with a young woman, usually clad in a very small, black thong bikini, as small as prudence and the FCC would allow. While the young lady draped herself sensuously over one of the fire-engine red Civics Hugo was selling, Hugo would yell at the top of his lungs, "Come on down. This is what you're gonna get." He would then point in the direction of the car and the bikini–clad woman.

These commercials apparently worked. Gorley had read in the Miami newspapers that Hugo had built himself a large home on Fisher Island, just off the coast of Miami. Hugo was famous for his lavish pool parties, often with B-List celebrities gracing the pool area which was surrounded by statutes of nude women, one of whom was said to be modeled on his ex-wife.

Not bad for a car dealer, who had originally started out selling the ill-fated and ill-designed Yugo in the early 1980s under the catchy name, "Hugo's Yugos." Those Yugos had disintegrated almost as soon as the buyer left the car lot and Time Magazine had listed it as one of the worst cars ever made. Hugo had filed for bankruptcy when the Yugo boom crashed, but somehow he was able to dig himself out of the hole and now was "on top of the world," in a favorite phrase of his. There were rumors around Miami that he had help from the mob and used his dealerships for laundering drug money.

Yao Lin asked, "You are aware that the Mariner cruise line is going to be sold in the bankruptcy court?"

Gorley had read in the local legal journal that the entire cruise line and all of its four ships, including the Mardi Gras, were scheduled to be sold at auction in the bankruptcy court in Miami in a couple of months. It seems that the former CEO of Mariner, Mark Hamilton, had run the cruise line aground and it was sinking fast from all of its debts. Mariner had once been the premiere cruise line in the business. Over the years, the Mariner ships had taken hundreds of thousands of passengers across the Atlantic and to Mediterranean ports. Now it had lost its luster. Coupled with the downturn in book- ings the cruise line recently had seen as a result of the various problems aboard its ships, bankruptcy had been the only viable option.

Although the four ships of the Mariner line were definitely showing their age and would need significant updates to match the latest, new cruise ships, they all were structurally sound or as they sometimes say, they all had "good bones." The company was a relative bargain at the auction re- serve price of $200,000,000. Today, just one of the ships like the Mardi Gras alone would cost over $300,000,000 to build. Given that, $200,000,000 for the entire cruise line fleet was clearly a chance for someone with the wherewithal to make a killing.

"Yes, of course, everyone in South Florida knows about the problems that Mariner is facing and the bankruptcy," responded Gorley.

Yao continued: "My company is very inter- ested in acquiring the Mariner cruise line, but there are certain obstacles unfortunately that stand in our way."

"Obstacles," Gorley said. "What kind of obstacles?"

Yao paused before finally responding: "I prefer not to go into the details of those at present. In due time, I will provide you with the relevant information when it is necessary for you to know it. I will say that not all of the obstacles are legal ones, but we will work with you on those that are not legal issues and look for your guidance on those that are legal. For your exclusive services to our company, I am prepared to give you a retainer of one million dollars immediately if you agree to represent Shanghai Blue in connection with this matter. In addition, upon successful completion of the acquisition, we will pay you another five million dollars."

Gorley was astounded. That's an enormous amount of money for a retainer and for the total fee. Particularly, because he was not sure why he was being retained. Talk about a "pig in a poke." But Gorley had other considerations to think about.

At 55, Gorley appeared to be at the top of his game. He had enjoyed enormous success and prestige, particularly at the criminal bar, where he often represented accused murderers of the worst kind. He often boasted to friends and colleagues that he had saved more men from death row than Jesus Christ.

But something was bugging Gorley. He felt that his practice was beginning to slow down. There were too many lawyers all over Florida and the country fighting for legal business. In Florida alone there were almost one hundred thousand lawyers. And the number kept growing as more and more baby boomers retired to Florida. After a few years of endless golf, some of the retired lawyers decided to open a law practice there. Some of them even ran ads on television that mimicked his own.

And then there were as the missed opportunities for him as a legal commentator. He had recently seen the noted Los Angeles patent lawyer, Jay Burns, on the Ellen DeGeneres Show, holding forth on the latest high-profile, Florida murder case. Gorley was jealous. Not only hadn't he been asked to represent the defendant in the case, he hadn't even been asked to comment on the case. He grabbed the remote and clicked the television set off. "Jesus, that guy has no business being on television. As my old man used to say, he doesn't know 'shit from shinola' about the intricacies of criminal law."

Gorley still felt like he could beat all comers at trial, if given half the chance. But, recently, he also had missed out on getting a few high profile cases, losing them to some "Johnny Upstarts," who didn't charge as much as he did or maybe, advertised more. In a capital murder case, where the death penalty was a possibility, he would take nothing less than a quarter of a million dollars—upfront—as his fee. Now, he began to wonder whether he had priced himself out of the market.

Not only that, not everything is as it seemed in his personal life. His estate in Palm Beach which he had bought at the peak of the real estate market was now under water financially. And that Rolls

Royce he stood next to in his commercials--- it was leased and the lease was running out in just a few months. The other drain on his money was the alimony he was ordered to pay his first wife. The judge had ordered him to pay her some $60,000 a month for life or until she remarried. The joke around town among the lawyers was, "If Gorley is so damn smart, how come he owes his ex some $720,000 a year." If this matter succeeded, he could prove them all wrong.

"I definitely need to consider this very interesting offer," Gorley said after a brief pause. "That's a lot of money, of course, but it would help me with my consideration if I knew precisely what it is I would be doing."

"All in good time," Yao replied. "All in good time, Mr. Gorley," Yao repeated. "Is there anything further we need to talk about today at this time?" asked Yao.

Gorley thought for a moment, and then responded, "No, I think that is all for now in light of your conditions. I just need to think a little more closely about this matter. You must admit that it is a rather strange situation for a lawyer to find himself in."

Yao nodded very slightly and then got up from his seat at the head of the conference table and said, "Please let me know by tomorrow morning at the latest, whether you are willing to help us. Thank you for the Scotch. It was quite good."

"Yes, of course. I will let you know by 10:00 o'clock tomorrow."

"Very good, Mr. Gorley. I do hope you can

assist us in this matter. And, by the way, please do not speak to anyone about our meeting. It is very important that this matter be kept quiet for the time being. I know that you are a man of discretion and would not betray the trust of your potential and, I hope, actual client."

"Yes, of course, the attorney client privilege applies to all of our discussions, so I am duty-bound not to reveal to anyone any of the information you have provided me. This is true even if we are unable to reach agreement on my representation."

"I thought so," responded Yao as Gorley escorted Yao and the others out of the conference room.

"I will wait to hear from you," said Yao as the group entered the lobby elevator and the elevator doors closed behind them. Gorley was sure that Sun Li winked at him behind those dark sunglasses, but of course, it was impossible to say for sure.

7

After his meeting with Yao Lin, Bud Gorley sat for a long time at his desk, looking out of his window at the Miami skyline, contemplating the proposal from the Chinese. He was worried because he did not know what exactly he would be asked to do. He felt a little like that undertaker in the first Godfather movie, who asks a favor from the Godfather, Don Corleone, on the occasion of his daughter's wedding. The Godfather grants the favor but says to him, "Someday—and that day may never come— I'll call upon you to do a service for me." The comment seemed to scare the bejesus out of the undertaker, but he was already in too deep to say anything except to agree. Gorley was scared also, but wondered if he also was already in too deep. Then he thought about the money they were offering. That thought alone convinced him that he had no choice but to take on this matter for the Chinese, regardless of what they would ask him to do. This Yao seemed like a reasonable man. It was unlikely he would ask Gorley to do anything that he could not handle. In any event, this would not be the first time he had done something risky. In some respects, his whole legal career had been based on risk taking of various sorts.

One of the first risks he had taken was one he had taken shortly after he had graduated from law school. Gorley was having a very difficult time building a legal practice. Like many young lawyers who are not hired by a large law firm as an associate, he had to scramble for clients as best he could. Although, according to the rules of professional ethics, lawyers are not supposed to solicit clients directly, Gorley decided he had to ignore that admonition if he was going to build a law practice out of nothing. Most people have heard of "ambulance chasers," lawyers who chase after ambulances from a crash scene in order to get clients injured in the crash. Gorley refined that technique. He would watch the local news on television and when there was a report of a major accident he would rush to the hospital to sign up the injured persons to contingency fee agreement. In one instance, Gorley had gone to the hospital to solicit business from a badly injured fireman who had just been brought in after a fall through the roof of a Wal-Mart. Contacting an injured party still in the hospital is a big 'no-no' for lawyers. In the hospital, while undergoing treatment for a broken back, the fireman signed a contingency fee agreement with Gorley, which gave Gorley 50% of any recovery against Wal-Mart and the roofing company, whether by settlement or verdict at trial. Gorley eventually did settle the fireman's claims for $1 million, but when the fireman realized that Gorley was to get half of the recovery, he retained another lawyer who complained to the state attorney disciplinary board and sued Gorley.

For the young Gorley, this had been just business as usual. The Florida Supreme Court Board of Discipline took a different view of that incident. The Board fined Gorley $25,000 and suspended him from the practice of law in Florida for a period of six months.

But that did not stop Gorley from using that tactic again and again to build his legal practice. "That was just the cost of doing business," Gorley later told his friends and added, "and it's a lot cheaper than those damn ads I run on local TV."

Gorley had told Yao that he would need to think it over, but as he sat there at his desk, he began to become concerned that if he did not act quickly enough, the Chinese might shop the matter along to another lawyer. Gorley could not let that happen. He picked up the phone and called the number Yao had given him.

"Mr. Yao, this is Bud Gorley," he said into the phone.

"Yes, Mr. Gorley, I was expecting your call. Can we do business together?"

Gorley paused for a moment before responding: "Yes, I think I can help you with your problem."

"Excellent," said Yao in response. "We will be in touch."

With that the phone went dead.

Even though it was now only 1 p.m., Gorley decided it was time to go home for the day since he did not think he could accomplish much more that day. He told his assistant, Avery, that he was not feeling well and took the elevator to the garage floor of the building. As he climbed into his Porsche Carrera in his reserved spot in the parking lot, he had the distinct impression that someone was watching him. He looked around in all directions but did not see anyone. He drove quickly out of the parking garage and stopped at the corner just outside the garage to see if anyone was following him. He sat there for a full two minutes but he saw no one else exiting the garage. He then put the Porsche in gear and sped off towards his house in Palm Beach. It was a long drive, some seventy miles each way, but he enjoyed it; it gave him time to clear his mind. But not today.

"I'm just being paranoid," Gorley said to himself as he gunned the Porsche down U.S. Highway 1. "It's crazy. Just crazy."

As he was pulling into his gated driveway, he stopped the car and looked around again just to make sure no one was following him. There was not another car in sight. He hurriedly closed the gate behind him and pulled into his garage.

About a block away, a black Range Rover with heavily-darkened windows turned the corner and pulled to the curb just as the gate to Gorley's mansion clanged shut. Inside the Range Rover were the two men who had accompanied Yao to Gorley's office.. Yao was taking every precaution. He needed to keep an eye on Gorley. There was just too much at stake here.

As Gorley was entering his house, he saw a package waiting on the doorstep. It was addressed to him and had a return address label from Shanghai Blue. He wondered how it got there since the gate to his estate had been locked when he arrived home. Somewhat warily, after he got inside his house, he opened the package. Inside the large box were neatly-bundled stacks of hundred dollar bills. So this Yao guy is for real, Gorley thought to himself.

Gorley never expected to receive the money

for the retainer in cash. But there it was. He took the box into his den. Fortunately neither his wife nor his children were home. It took him over an hour to count the money. It was all there: one million dollars. That million would go a long way in solving some of his financial problems. Not all the way, he knew, but certainly it was a start.

Then Gorley realized he had a problem: What to do with the money? He knew that if he just took it to the bank, the bank would have to report the deposit to the U.S. Treasury Department because under banking regulations designed to deter money laundering, any transaction involving more than ten thousand dollars in cash had to be reported. Then he remembered that he and his wife had recently rented a storage locker at a facility not far from their house. He took the box and put it in the trunk of his Rolls and drove there. He felt more than a little strange as he opened the locker and placed the box of money in a corner atop a marble-topped table that his wife had taken there recently since it was no longer in style. Before leaving the locker, he removed ten stacks of hundred dollar bills and placed them in a brief case he had brought along. Each stack contained ten thousand dollars. "Walking around money," Gorley laughed to himself as he drove back home.

The Range Rover with the darkened windows was not too far behind him.

Gorley wondered what Yao would ask him to do to earn this huge retainer. He knew it would not be easy. But whatever the job, Gorley knew he would have to do it.

8

Two weeks after his meeting with Mr. Yao, Gorley received a phone call from Yao.

"Mr. Gorley, this is Yao Lin."

"Hello Yao, very good to hear from you again," Gorley lied, hoping that Yao did not notice the slight tremor in his voice.

"You will recall that when we last spoke, I told you that we would be calling upon you for some work in clearing obstacles for us in connection with our acquisition of the Mariner cruise line."

"Yes, yes, of course."

"You will recall that I mentioned the Mardi Gras cruise ship?"

"Yes," Gorley said.

"I wanted to let you know that the Mardi Gras will be leaving Miami in a couple of days for its weekly cruise to Cozumel, Mexico. Shortly before it returns to port at the end of the week, I will contact you again about your representation and provide you with the necessary details for what we will need you to do. Make sure that you are ready."

With that, Yao hung up the phone before Gorley could say a word.

"What the hell is this all about?" Gorley thought. "What have I gotten myself into?"

9

Before proceeding with my interviews concerning Mrs. Weigand's disappearance, I wanted to examine the Weigand suite on the Empress deck to see if there was any evidence that might aid in the investigation. I asked Captain Vivaldi and Dragan, the second officer, to accompany me. The suite that the Weigands occupied was located in the middle of the ship, not far from the guest services counter. Dragan had obtained the key to the suite from housekeeping and we entered without knocking. The suite was clearly unoccupied and neat as a pin. I poked around every part of the two large rooms that made up the suite. Together they were about triple the size of my own cabin and at least double the size of most of the cabins on the ship. As far as I could see, there was nothing out of the ordinary and certainly I saw no evidence of a struggle having taken place in the rooms. In fact, it appeared to me as though the rooms had never even been used recently.

"So, this is the potential crime scene?" I said. "Has someone cleaned it up?"

"We think the steward did clean up the rooms this morning as he would normally do," answered Dragan.

"That's not very helpful, is it? If there was any evidence of a crime here, it is probably gone now."

"I will have to look into that, Lieutenant," responded Dragan rather defensively as he made a note in a small notebook he always carried with him.

"There is nothing here that I can see to indicate there has been a murder in this cabin. But I'll want to talk to the steward to find out if he saw anything in the room this morning that might be helpful."

I could see that Captain Vivaldi was quite agitated when I said this.

"I'm not sure why you are focusing on the Weigands' suite," Vivaldi said. "You don't believe that Robert had anything to do with his wife's disappearance, do you? I have spoken to Mr. Weigand since we first met earlier this morning. He says he believes his wife has been murdered. He denies knowing anything about her disappearance and of course he denies having anything to do with her disappearance. He has no other explanation for why she is now missing. I must say that I believe him. Why would a woman disappear on her honeymoon? Nothing else makes any sense to him or to me."

"Where is Weigand now?" I asked

"I thought it best under the circumstances to keep him in my cabin. He is, as you might imagine, very distraught."

I knew that in most cases when a woman is murdered or turns up missing, the husband or boyfriend is always the prime suspect. Surely, the Captain also knew this. And why was Vivaldi so deeply involved in protecting Weigand? I thought it was very unusual.

"Where is the Hugo cabin?" I asked Dragan.

"Next door," said Dragan.

"Next door? Are you sure?"

"Quite sure."

"Isn't that rather strange, that Hugo would be right next door to the honeymoon couple?"

"I will look into that, sir," said Dragan as he made another entry in his notebook.

"While we are here, let's take a look at that cabin as well since Weigand claims he heard an argument there last night."

I knocked on the door of the Hugo suite, but no one answered the door. Neither the Captain nor Dragan had a key to Hugo's suite, so that my examination of the Hugo suite would have to wait until later.

"I will come back later. I definitely want to see the cabin and speak to Mr. Hugo. For now, let's go up to the Captain's cabin so that I can talk to Mr. Weigand myself."

10

"Mr. Weigand," I began, "my name is Lieutenant Mario Morales, and I am the chief of security aboard this ship. I have a few questions I would like to ask you about exactly what happened to your wife. I understand she is missing. I have had the ship searched and she has not been found on board. Neither do the surveillance cameras show that she is or was in the water surrounding the ship. Maybe you can tell me exactly what happened last night and why she may have disappeared and why you think she has been murdered."

Weigand, who had been lying face down on the Captain's bed, raised his head up and turned slowly towards me. His eyes were red, apparently from crying, and he was completely disheveled. He looked as though he had slept in his clothes.

"I didn't do anything to her," Weigand moaned in a thin voice that cracked as he spoke.

"I didn't do anything to her," he repeated as he put his head down and began crying softly into the pillow.

Captain Vivaldi walked over to the bed and touching Weigand's shoulder, said, "Everything will be all right, Robert."

I decided I would no longer be so gentle with Weigand. I walked over to Weigand as he lay on the bed and said to him, "what happened to your wife? Did you kill her?"

Weigand rolled over, looked directly into my eyes and said quietly, "no, I have no idea what happened to her. I woke up and she just wasn't there." He then repeated the story that he had told Boudreaux, "I last saw her at the casino with Joe Hugo, our boss."

"Tell me exactly what you and your wife did all day yesterday," I said as I sat down at the Captain's desk. The top of the desk was almost entirely covered with newspapers, navigation charts, nautical instruments, a Vivaldi CD entitled "The Four Seasons" and a gun, partially covered by some of the navigation maps. The gun was a pearl handled revolver with six cylinders. It looked like a .45 caliber. I had suspected that the Captain probably had a gun on board the ship, but I would never have thought he would have such a fancy one as this one. It looked a lot like the one that General Patton wore during World War II in all those pictures of him. And more importantly, why was it sitting on top of the Captain's desk with this apparently desperate man in his bed? I quietly picked the gun up and placed it in my coat pocket. "I will have to talk to Tony about this," I said to myself.

"I really don't know where to begin," said Weigand as he regained his composure and sat up in the bed. "It all seems like a dream, or really, I guess, a nightmare. I just can't believe she is gone."

I listened quietly as Weigand told his story of what had happened that day before her disappearance. Quite simply, his story sounded like a quiet day on the ship that just about anyone could have experienced. He said they spent most of the day at the pool, had lunch in the adjoining dining room and dinner in the ship's gourmet Italian restaurant, Piccolina's. Afterwards, he said they had a few drinks in their suite. They decided to skip the Captain's welcoming party, but he said they did go to watch the magic show that was playing that evening in the ship's main auditorium. Following the show, they walked to the casino where he said he played a few hands of blackjack, losing several hundred dollars. He claimed that he left the casino around midnight, leaving his wife with his boss, Hugo. Weigand said he returned to his cabin and never saw or heard from his wife again.

I asked Weigand if his wife had been depressed. He denied it, saying she was in high spirits when he left her at the casino the night before. He said he felt she was in good hands with Mr. Hugo when he returned to his suite. Weigand expected his wife would be right along as the cards were bad that night and he thought she would soon lose the remainder of the money he had given her.

11

After I was done with my questioning of Weigand, I stepped out into the hall with Captain Vivaldi.

"Are you done with your interrogation?" he said to me.

"It was not an interrogation, Captain. I prefer to call it an interview. I am just trying to get a complete picture of what might have happened to Mrs. Weigand. Sometimes the most seemingly insignificant detail can lead to a solution. I do have one question for you that has been troubling me all morning. What is your relationship with Mr. Weigand? Obviously, from what I have seen, you know him quite well."

Captain Vivaldi turned and said to me, "He is my nephew. He is my sister's son."

So that explained why Weigand got this special treatment. Small world, indeed.

"Since he is your sister's son, tell me about him, what kind of man is he and is he the kind of guy who would kill his wife?"

The Captain appeared rather startled at the bluntness of my question and he answered unequivocally, "There is no way that Robert could have killed his wife or anyone else, for that matter."

"Convince me," I said. "And tell me how he ended up on his honeymoon cruise with his and his wife's boss, Joe Hugo. You've got to admit that the whole thing is rather odd."

The Captain then proceeded to tell me the story of how the Weigands had met and married. I had to admit that it was quite a story.

According to the Captain, Robert Weigand was a highly successful car salesman in Miami with Joe Hugo's main dealership. He was generally the salesman of the month and some months he would actually outsell all of the other salesmen in the dealership combined.

Linda Berkeley also worked for the same Hugo dealership in Miami. She had originally been hired about a year ago to work in the accounting department as a bookkeeper. She was tall and willowy with a flash of red hair that flowed down her back in large curls. Soon after she was hired, she caught the eye of Joe Hugo. Hugo decided she was too beautiful to work in accounting. Instead, he put her in his television commercials, which ran incessantly on the local television stations throughout Florida. In other words, she was the latest of his bikini-clad temptresses.

Not only had Linda caught the eye of Hugo, she also caught Weigand's eye. They began dating and soon moved in together in an apartment in South Beach. Several months later, Weigand asked Linda to marry him. The Captain told me that Weigand had been married before. He didn't know what happened to Weigand's first wife, but he thought that she had moved to Las Vegas, where she was to get a divorce. He said that he didn't know if she had actually obtained one. The Captain also did not know if Weigand had told Linda anything about his first wife. Hearing this, I began to wonder if it was possible that the first Mrs. Weigand had seen the wedding on television and had popped back up in Robert's life. I knew stranger things had happened to supply a motive for murder.

The Captain told me that when the couple told Hugo they were going to marry, at first, Hugo seemed quite sullen and upset. Both were very concerned that they might lose their jobs because Hugo had a no fraternization policy for his employees.

At this point, I interrupted the Captain and asked him, "What kind of relationship did Hugo have with Linda?"

The Captain paused and then answered, "They had been lovers," the Captain said, but their relationship was now all over according to Linda, who had confided in the Captain but specifically told him not to tell Robert.

"Did you tell Robert?" I asked.

"No, of course not. I would never betray her trust. Never."

I was surprised how adamant the Captain was in his denial, particularly because it was Robert who was his relation. I would have thought he might feel compelled to tell Robert.

The Captain continued with his story. He said about a week after their announcement that they were going to marry, Hugo's mood abruptly changed. Hugo told the couple that he wanted them to have the wedding at the Honda dealership and shown on live television. "Just like Kate and Wills," Hugo said. "It will be fit for a King and Queen," he told them.

"It will be great publicity for the dealership, of course," Hugo also said to them. He added, "And it will save you a lot of money because I will pay for everything, including the honeymoon." The Captain said that they reluctantly agreed to this bizarre request in order to keep their jobs.

According to the Captain, the wedding was quite an extravagant affair. On the day of the wedding, some two thousand people crowded into the dealership to see the wedding. The wedding had been highly publicized in the news media prior to the wedding and several local television stations had sent crews to cover the wedding itself. Hugo was counting on a number of those people to buy new Hondas and he was not disappointed as it was the biggest sales day in the history of the dealership. The showroom was decorated in white bunting throughout and there were piles upon piles of white gardenias everywhere. Some of the people were heard complaining that because of all the flowers and the damp, humid weather, the showroom smelled a bit like a funeral home.

Hugo even was ordained as a Universal Life minister so that he could officiate at their wedding. He had read about the Universal Life church in Time Magazine and was surprised to learn that all he had to do to be ordained was to fill out an online application. Hugo wondered if he could now claim clergyman status at his country club in Jupiter, Florida where he loved to golf.

The wedding ceremony lasted only a few minutes. At the reception that followed, each of the guests/customers was given a small glass of champagne and a slice of the wedding cake, an almond torte, especially created for the occasion by one of the Food Network pastry chefs. The cake alone had cost Hugo over $3000. It was nothing, however, compared to what he made that day selling cars.

As a wedding present, Hugo gave the couple two tickets for a cruise to Cozumel, Mexico aboard the Mardi Gras. He promised them the trip of a lifetime. When he told them he would be joining them on the cruise, the Captain said that they were startled, but they had no choice but to go along with it.

When the Captain finished his story, I said to him, "That is a very odd scenario, very odd."

The Captain's only comments were, "Perhaps, perhaps."

"One last thing," I said. "I found this pearl-handled revolver on your desk under a stack of papers." When I pulled the gun from my pocket to show him, he looked rather frightened.

"What was that doing on my desk?" the Captain asked.

"I was about to ask you the same question," I responded. "It's not your gun, I take it?"

"No, of course not. I usually do not like to have firearms aboard my ship. When I was in the Merchant Marine we were never permitted to have arms aboard ship. I thought that was a good policy and I have carried it over to this ship."

"So, whose gun is it and how did it get into your room?" I asked.

"I have no idea. The only thing I can think of is that it must belong to Robert. I can't believe it. But maybe he was thinking of taking his own life. Thank God you found the gun and took it away."

"Perhaps," I said. "Perhaps. If it is his gun,

that is very interesting. And if he was intending to kill himself, why?"

Maybe we had just discovered the prime suspect. But what was the motivation? Had Mrs. Weigand found out about the first Mrs. Weigand?

12

After I had finished my interview with Weigand, I returned to my cabin. I sat down at my desk, mulling over what Weigand and the Captain had just told me. At this stage of the investigation, nothing was clear to me. I looked at the clock on the small table next to my bed. It was now almost nine o'clock and ship was beginning to come alive as it always did around that time.

As I was sitting there, mulling all of what had happened so far that morning, I heard a knock on the door of my cabin.

"Who is it?"

"Sergeant Boudreaux."

"What do you want?"

"Lieutenant Morales, I need to talk to about this murder investigation. I think I know what happened to Mrs. Weigand."

"Come in, "I said.

Boudreaux then opened the door and entered the cabin.

"So, you say you have information about what happened to Mrs. Weigand," I began. "As you know, I am yet to be convinced that she was murdered. Certainly, we have a distraught husband and a missing wife. But no body and no evidence that would suggest foul play. It is possible that she jumped or fell overboard, I grant you. But there is no hard evidence of that either. All we have so far is a lot of speculation. I needed some time to think about this so-called murder before I spoke with you.

But now I am glad you are here so that we can discuss this matter together."

"I disagree, Lieutenant," Sergeant Boudreaux began. "I believe that there has been a murder and that Joe Hugo is responsible for that murder."

"Hugo, why Hugo? What motive did he have to kill her?"

"I think Hugo was having an affair with Mrs. Weigand before she married Weigand."

"So I have been told," I said. "I also remembered having seen those television commercials that Hugo runs, where he nuzzles Mrs. Weigand or some other woman while trying to sell his cars. They seemed just a little too friendly not to suspect that something is going on between them. But she decided to marry Weigand. So?"

"That's just it," said Boudreaux. "I think she broke it off with Hugo but he wouldn't let her go. I think she went to Hugo's cabin with him last night after they left the casino. He probably gave her a drink or two and then tried to force her to have sex with him. She wouldn't play along with Hugo's game. They then had a fight and he killed her. QED."

"That's very interesting. If that is what happened, where is the body? You are like a lot of cops I've known over the years, ready to convict the first person you think is responsible even though you have no real facts."

Boudreaux turned quite red in the face as she responded: "I believe Hugo dumped the body overboard, thinking she will never be found and he will be in the clear."

I rubbed my chin as I responded. "If that's what happened, there should be video from the security cameras showing the two of them together and maybe even one of Hugo dumping the body overboard, wouldn't there?"

Closed circuit television cameras are mounted on every corridor and in the various public rooms throughout the ship. Most passengers are photographed multiple times during the course of a cruise. Other than the staterooms, there are few places aboard ship that are not covered by security cameras.

"Yes, of course. I have already looked at the tapes from last night and I have spoken to the crew about Hugo."

"So, what is it that exactly that you saw on the surveillance tapes and learned from the crew," I asked.

"It seems that the suite next door to the Weigands' suite was Hugo's personal playpen."

"What the hell does that mean?"

"It means that was where he brought women for a little fun and games. Some of those games, I was told, were quite unusual. Bondage, masochistic stuff. You know, the 'Fifty Shades of Grey' stuff everyone is talking about these days."

"Are you sure about all of this?"

"I am. Positive."

"How come you are so sure of all of this?"

"Hugo is a frequent cruiser on the Mariner ships and, particularly on the Mardi Gras. Let's just say everyone on the crew knows what's going on

66 · AJ BASINSKI

with Mr. Hugo and his friends. Apparently, Hugo had seduced several young women in his cabin."

"Everyone knew about this but me, it seems," I said, shaking my head. "Everyone but me," I repeated.

"And what about the security tapes, what do they show?"

"The camera mounted on the hall where Hugo's cabin was located shows Hugo and Linda Weigand going into Hugo's cabin around one o'clock this morning There is another tape that I think shows Hugo leaving the cabin several hours later carrying a black trash bag. Another camera on the port side of the ship around the same time shows a man throwing what looks like a black bag overboard. There is no video showing Linda Weigand ever leaving Hugo's suite. I believe she was in that black bag or at least her body was in the bag."

"Quite a story, Sergeant. I will want to see those tapes for myself, of course. If you are correct, those tapes would appear to be very powerful evidence against Mr. Hugo. Are you certain that it is Hugo carrying the bag and throwing it overboard?"

"Well, those tapes are quite blurry due to the poor lighting inside and the fog outside, but who else could it be, coming out of his suite? And who else would be throwing a bag overboard?"

"Good questions, Sergeant," I responded. "As I said before, shouldn't we have all the facts before we jump to any conclusions about a murder and who was the murderer?"

"It seems pretty obvious to me, Lieutenant," said Sergeant Boudreaux. I could tell that she was quite disgusted with me now.

As she prepared to leave my office, she turned and said to me, "I almost forgot to tell you, but I also spoke briefly with Mr. Hugo morning."

I was irritated that she had already done this without my permission but decided to ignore this new breach of protocol for now and asked her, "And what did he say?"

"He denied having anything to do with her murder or disappearance, as you continue to call it. But he did say he had heard some noise last night from the Weigands' cabin. Said it sounded like a gunshot."

"Very interesting. Well, Sergeant, doesn't that put a very different perspective on this whole matter? I will speak with him shortly myself. Thank you, Sergeant."

"It would, except I didn't believe a word that man said. I think he made the whole thing up to throw suspicion on Weigand. And I understand from Dragan that you have already seen the Weigands' suite and he said it was clean as a whistle. Don't you think there would have been some evidence of a gunshot or blood?"

"You are right, of course, Sergeant, but for one thing. The suite had already been cleaned by the steward early this morning for some ungodly reason and the evidence may have already been lost. I am sure that when we dock, the FBI or the Dade County sheriff will want to run some more sophisticated tests on that suite to determine the presence of blood and gunshot residue. We, of course, lack the equipment aboard the ship to do so. I have ordered

Dragan to quarantine the suite until they have a chance to do so. And one more thing, Sergeant, when I was interviewing Mr. Weigand in the Captain's suite I came across this revolver."

I pulled the gun from my desk drawer and showed it to Boudreaux.

"When I found it, I asked the Captain if it was his. He denied that it was, but even he speculated that it might be Weigand's. And you know, of course, that Weigand is his nephew." Boudreaux seemed quite startled as I said this.

"When we dock, I will hand the gun over to the FBI so that the gun can be tested to see if it was fired recently. I'm sure then we may have some facts to deal with."

To me this was still a case of disappearance. I did not want any pre-conceived ideas to interfere with my investigation. That was something that I was always trying to do: keeping an open mind particularly at the beginning of an investigation and not focus on just one man or woman. I had seen this happen all too often that when the police focused on just one suspect, they actually ignored a lot of the facts and evidence which suggested the guilt of someone else. Basically, they did not want to hear it once they had made up their minds as to who they believed was the guilty party or how the crime was committed. And the prosecutors, they were just as bad, if not worse. They would often adopt the police theories without doing their own research or investigation. During my time on the LAPD, I tried to look at all the evidence before making any conclusions concerning the guilt or innocence of any individual. And more oftentimes than not, I was right. The problem now was that there was no evidence at all except for those tapes that Sergeant Boudreaux had viewed. Those tapes might indeed hold the key to the solution of Mrs. Weigand's disappearance. But then again, they may not. I need to see and analyze them myself.

13

It was now almost 10 a.m. and the rising sun had burned off the thick fog and ship was underway again. My next step in the investigation was to interview Joe Hugo. I felt I had gathered enough information to make it an informed interview and not just a series of accusations. As I was on my way to Hugo's suite, I passed the dining room and decided to stop in for a cup of coffee. It had already been a long morning. Fortunately my hangover was now gone. But I was sure that, from what I had heard about Hugo and seen on television, he would turn out to be a real piece of work. But was he a murderer? That was at the top of my mindset: I would need to gauge whether he was capable of murder. I thought a cup of coffee might help.

As I crossed the Lido deck which I had searched just a few hours before, I walked past the large kidney shaped pool in the middle of the deck. I could hear the clang of dishes being laid out in the dining room. I could also smell the bacon and eggs being prepared by the chefs for the onslaught of guests who were already beginning to fill every chair of the dining room and the area around the pool. A few couples with children had staked out their spots in lounge chairs around the hot tub near the pool by laying blue Mariner beach towels on them. A young couple, probably newly married, huddled in the shade as the sun began its slow climb above the top deck of the ship as it steamed along, trailing black smoke from the enormous stacks that towered over the rest of the ship. Emblazoned on both sides of the tallest stack was the picture of an albatross which was the logo of the Mariner cruise line. When I first saw the albatross, I though it meant bad luck. Like a lot of people who have read Samuel Taylor Coleridge's "The Rime of the Ancient Mariner", I remembered the disasters that befell a sailor who had shot an albatross and had it wrapped around his neck. But, I learned that in reality the albatross is considered to be good luck and that it is only when it is harmed that it brings on the bad luck. I only hoped that was true.

It had been a difficult morning. Yet I felt that I was no further along in finding out what happened to Linda Weigand than several hours ago when I was awakened by the knock on my door.

When I got to the dining room, I saw Captain Vivaldi in the corner farthest from the door. He already had a large cup of coffee in front of him as he pored over some papers spread out over the table. When Vivaldi saw me, he gathered up the papers, stood up and quickly left the dining room.

"What was that all about?" I wondered as I drew down a large cup of coffee from the coffee urn in the middle of the dining room. I sat down at a table on the port side of the ship next to an open window so I could get some fresh air. It was now a clear morning and it was already quite warm.

"May I join you?" asked a young lady as I was finishing my coffee.

"But, of course," I said as I looked up at her. I recognized her immediately as the young Asian lady I had been drinking tequila with at the Captain's party the night before. Things were beginning to look up on this otherwise depressing morning.

"My name is Sun Li," the young lady said as she reached across the table to shake my hand.

"Mario Morales," I said as nonchalantly as I could as I reached across the table to meet her hand. My heart began pounding in my ear as I did this.

When my hand touched hers, I could feel that it was soft and I could smell her perfume or rose water. She was even more beautiful than I had remembered from the night before. Large, round sunglasses shielded her eyes.

"I don't know if you remember me," she said as she sat down at the table. How could I possibly have forgotten this little lotus blossom

"Of course I remember you." I said to this enchantress in front of me now. "We sat together at the Captain's dinner last night. We both had quite a bit to drink. Tequila was your drink of choice, if I recall correctly."

"Yes, I know. It was a very nice dinner. I really enjoyed myself. Maybe a little too much. I don't know about you, but I had quite a hangover this morning."

I laughed and said, "Ditto on this end."

She smiled and said, "If I remember right, you work on the ship, don't you?"

I wasn't quite sure what I had told her the night before since I sometimes did not want to let people know my real position, but I decided I had better tell her the truth now.

"Yes "I said. "I am in charge of security aboard the Mardi Gras."

"Then," she said, "you can tell me what happened this morning."

"What happened this morning?" I asked, perhaps a bit too eagerly.

"Don't tell me you didn't hear about the murder?"

I was flabbergasted. Had someone already told the passengers about the Weigand disappearance?

"I'm not sure I know what you are talking about," I said somewhat defensively.

"Early this morning I was in my room and around 5 am, I heard a noise in the hall and someone was shouting about a 'murder'."

Damn that Roman, I thought. He was so loud when he came knocking on my door that probably half the ship now knew about the disappearance of Mrs. Weigand.

"Yes, I am familiar with what you are talking about," I said. "We believe that it may have been a college prank, but we are still looking into the matter. Rest assured, Ms. Sun, this ship is as safe as it can be. Here, let me give you my card. If you should ever have any concerns about anything aboard the ship, please feel free to call me."

"That's good to know," said the young lady as she pushed away from the table and started walking away. "It was nice talking to you and good luck with your discovery of the pranksters. I am sure you will find out who did it."

I wanted to cry out, "Wait, don't go. I want to know you better and spend time with you." Of course I said nothing of the kind. I never did.

I did get up from the table and I tried to follow her out of the dining room, but a large number of people suddenly came into the dining area and I lost her in the crowd. I said to myself that I will have to check the ship's passenger list to see what cabin Sun Li is in. At least I now know her name.

14

When I got back to my office, I checked the ship's passengers list. There was no one named Sun Li listed as being on board. I checked it again for variations on the name, but nothing even close turned up.

Very strange, I mused. Very strange.

There was a knock on the door as I turned off the computer. "Who is it," I shouted.

"Virginia Boudreaux," came the response.

Just what I needed right now. Despite my misgivings about talking to her again, I walked to the door and let her in.

"Do you have any idea what is happening on this ship?" she virtually shouted at me. "There are all kinds of rumors floating around about murders and gangs of thieves roaming the ship. You know how everything gets blown out of proportion once these rumors surface. And you sit here in your office, playing video games, no doubt."

"Actually, I was checking out a potential lead, Sergeant" I said very calmly.

"A lead, what kind of lead?" Boudreaux snapped.

"I just talked to a young lady at breakfast in the dining room. She claimed that her name was Sun Li, but when I checked the ship's passenger list no one is listed with that name. She seemed to know quite a bit about what may have happened to Mrs. Weigand, referring at one point to a murder. Said she heard something in the hall last night about a murder. What she may have heard, I suspect, was Roman announcing to me that there was a murder when he woke me up at 5 a.m. But I also got the feeling that she knew a lot more than that. I suspect that Sun Li or whatever her real name is, may be responsible for all these rumors you are talking about. By the way, Sergeant," I concluded, "I don't even know how to play video games."

15

It was now early afternoon and I knew now was the time I had to talk to Hugo myself. I walked down the hall to Hugo's suite. I knocked on the door and I was surprised when it was opened by a tall man with a mustache and gray hair. He reminded me of Alfred, the butler for Bruce Wayne, Batman. He was wearing tails, a black morning coat, and the full bridegroom regalia. Except this was no groom. I quickly realized that he must be Hugo's butler. I had never seen a butler before on the ship or anywhere else for that matter. I guess I just didn't travel in those kinds of circles. Obviously, Joe Hugo did.

"Lieutenant Morales to see Mr. Hugo," I said as I stepped into the cabin. I had never seen this particular suite before. It was luxurious to say the least. Everything in the front room looked as though it came directly from an Ethan Allen furniture showroom. There was even a small piano, a Steinway no less, in one corner of the suite. Very impressive.

As I entered the cabin, I heard someone yell out, "Is that room service with my lunch? It's about time. Tell the boy that I will be right out."

A man I presumed to be Hugo came out of the suite's bathroom a minute or so later. He was dressed in a large white bathrobe with his name in blue letters on the right side of the robe as well as some sort of crest. Maybe his family crest, I laughed to myself.

"Over here, boy. I'll take my lunch over

here" he motioned to me as he sat down on the large, brown leather couch that dominated the room. "Just put it on this table right here," he said as he pointed to the large, rectangular coffee table in front of the couch. At the same time, he switched on the large screen television across the room. ESPN's Sports Center came on with the usual chatter about everything related to sports.

Before I could respond to Hugo, the butler jumped in and said, rather nervously, "I'm afraid that is not your lunch, sir. It should be here momentarily. This is Lieutenant Morales, sir. He wishes to speak to you about a matter. I am sure that your lunch will be here shortly." He had a distinct English accent and I wondered how Hugo had found him.

"Lieutenant Morales, who the hell is that?"

"I am the ship's head of security," I said.

"I thought you were one of those Filipino boys bringing up my lunch. Andre, check on that and make sure he gets here chop, chop. You know how I hate to miss a meal and how cranky I get when I do."

Andre disappeared into the adjoining room and Hugo motioned to me to sit down on the bright, yellow couch in the middle of the suite, opposite to the couch where he was sitting. He then flicked off the television.

I was surprised at Hugo's appearance. He was unshaven, even though it was now the middle of the day and he was still in his pajamas. He also looked much more mild-mannered than he did on television in those ads that ran incessantly on local stations in South Florida. In those he always seemed to me to be like a caged tiger ready to explode.

Hugo asked me if I would like something to drink.

"No, I think I'm fine," I responded. At the same time, I was actually thinking, I would like to have a rum and coke, but decided it would be unseemly to do so under the circumstances. I watched, however, as Hugo got up from the couch and went over to and behind the small bar in the corner of the cabin and poured himself 2 inches of Jack Daniels and tossed exactly three ice cubes into the glass.

"What can I do for you, Lieutenant? Sure you don't want a drink?" Hugo said. "Sorry, I didn't know who you were when you came in. But you have got to understand, as I'm sure you know, all you boys look alike."

It took a lot of will power, but I held my tongue at this remark. I knew it would not help to lose my temper over a crack like that about my ethnic background from this oaf. I had heard a lot worse when I was a cop with the LAPD, particularly after I had become a Lieutenant. A lot worse, believe me. And some of it from my fellow cops. I waited a moment to gather my composure and then said, "I'm here as part of my investigation of the Weigand matter."

"I spoke to a young lady earlier today and told her all I knew. She was quite pretty, by the way. And quite a rack. She said she was involved with security also. You getting any of that?"

"That would have been Sergeant Boudreaux," I said.

"You mean like the fine wine? She did have a fine little ass on her also."

"I'm not here to talk about the finer points of Ms. Boudreaux' body parts. I need to know what you know about the disappearance of Mrs. Weigand. And by the way, Mr. Hugo, her name is Boudreaux, not Bordeaux, like the wine. I understand that you were the employer of both Mr. and Mrs. Weigand. Wasn't it a little unusual for you to accompany them on their honeymoon?"

"Let's just say that I wanted to look after my investment," Hugo replied. "These were my two best employees and I had generously spent quite a lot of money on their wedding. It was beautiful. Captain Vivaldi was there, by the way and had a great time. You would have enjoyed it, also, Lieutenant."

"I'm sure that I would have, Mr. Hugo, but the question I have for you is: What do you know about the disappearance of Mrs. Weigand?" I thought it best to confront Hugo directly and get his reaction, so I added what I had already been told: "I understand you spent some time with her in the casino last night. In fact, you may well have been the last person to actually see her last night." Of course, I did not mention anything about the surveillance tapes that Boudreaux had seen. No reason to reveal all that to him now.

Hugo was very calm as he answered. "Yes, I saw her last night. Beautiful gal. She was very much alive when I left her. And, of course, I know nothing about her disappearance or whatever it is that happened to her. I am very sorry to hear about it, as you might imagine. She was a very good employee, almost like a daughter to me. And Robert, of course, he is our very best salesman. I would hate to lose him over this tragedy. I told your young lady that I heard what sounded like a gunshot last night and it may have come from the cabin next door. I don't know for sure. That's all I know, Lieutenant. It was probably nothing but a television on too loud. I don't know."

I thought it unusual that Hugo would refer not only to Linda's disappearance but also say that he did not know "whatever it is that happened to her." I pulled out my notebook from my pocket and made a note of that statement because I thought that someday it could be very important to the investigation. At this stage of the investigation, who knows what is important and what isn't? That's the beauty of keeping an open mind and not jumping too soon to any conclusions as to the guilt or innocence of any party.

"Did you have anything to do with Mrs. Weigand's disappearance, Mr. Hugo? " I persisted.

Suddenly, Hugo was a changed man. "Lieutenant," he said, "I told your pretty little sergeant what I knew. I heard some noise that could have been a gunshot and that was it. Why would you think I knew anything more about that matter? I think that is all I have to say for now. And quit pestering everyone about this. You got that, Morales."

I was nonplused at this abrupt change in his demeanor. I had not expected this type of reaction from Hugo.

"Mr. Hugo, there has been the disappearance and perhaps the murder of a woman on this ship, a woman who you may have been the last person to see alive. It is my job to investigate and find out exactly what happened to her, I would think that you would also want to get to the bottom of this, particularly because she was your employee and you knew her rather well."

"You know, Morales, let me tell you something," Hugo's voice was rising several octaves as he spoke, reminding me of those television commercials he ran where he screamed at the audience. "Pretty damn soon, you will be working for me. I am in the process of buying the Mariner cruise line so this ship will soon belong to me and so will you when we get back to Miami for the closing on the deal. Of course the closing is just a formality. So keep that in mind as you conduct your investigation."

Very interesting, I thought. I had known that the Mariner cruise line was in bankruptcy but had no idea that Hugo was going to buy Mariner out of bankruptcy. I had heard that the Chinese were interested in getting into the cruise line business and thought that they might end up buying the Mariner line. Increasingly, I had seen large numbers of Chinese passengers on the ship. Somewhere I had read that more Chinese went on overseas trips than Americans—some 70 million Chinese. In fact, earlier in the year, I had read in the Wall Street Journal about a Chinese company that had entered into the cruise market. The article stated that China's first luxury cruise ship, Henna, made her maiden voyage from Sanya Phoenix Island International Port in late January. It was owned by one of those new Chinese billionaires, Fong Gee

"You may be my future employer or, as you say, own me in the future," I said, "But until the deal closes and you do with me as you choose, I am still the head of security on this ship and I will conduct my investigation my way to find out what happened to Mrs. Weigand. Once you own the ship, you can do whatever the hell you want with me. Until then, I will proceed to get to the bottom of this whole matter."

Hugo turned away, but remained silent. It seemed like an eternity, although it was only a few seconds. I knew I was being dismissed, so I got off the couch and walked to the door. Andre, the butler, was there to open the door for me. Just outside was the Filipino steward with Hugo's lunch.

"Have a good day, Mr. Hugo," I said as I left the suite.

As I began walking down the hall, I heard Hugo bellow, "Forget about the damn lunch. Just forget about it. Get me my damn lawyer in Miami. Who does that boy think he is?"

The door to Hugo's cabin slammed shut behind me.

16

When I returned to my security office after my meeting with Hugo, I found a yellow Post-It note stuck on the door. It was from someone named Ken Hendricks. I had never heard of him. The handwritten note read as follows:

"Dear Lieutenant Morales, I am a reporter for the Miami Tribune-Gazette and I have been asked by my editor to investigate the series of recent problems such as fires, disappearances and other mishaps, aboard the Mariner Cruise line ships, and particularly aboard the Mardi Gras. I would very much appreciate an opportunity to talk to you about these matters before I do any further interviews. I am located in stateroom 407. Please come by my room as soon as possible."

It was signed, "Ken Hendricks." There was also a short postscript at the bottom of the note that read:

"I understand that there was a murder aboard the ship last night. It is urgent I speak with you."

"Holy Christ," I groaned as I finished reading the note and threw it on my desk. "The whole damn world knows about this Weigand investigation." I decided I had better find this Hendricks guy and learn what he really knows and who he talked to. With a newspaper reporter involved, the whole situation could completely spiral out of control. And maybe it already had.

17

Ken Hendricks was an investigative reporter for the Miami Tribune-Gazette, an upstart city paper that was given away for free at Starbucks, fast food restaurants and on street corners in Miami and the surrounding towns and suburbs. Bill Wright, the publisher and editor-in-chief of the newspaper, had inherited more money than he knew what to do with, so he started the newspaper. He viewed himself as sort of a muckraker of the old school of journalism.

Hendricks was Wright's best reporter. Hendricks had worked for newspapers in Cincinnati and Pittsburgh before he moved to Florida to get away from the cold weather. Since he had joined the staff of the Miami Tribune-Gazette, he had written a number of incisive investigative stories. He even had received awards from local news organizations for several of his stories. At 31 years of age, he was definitely a comer in the field of journalism and some people felt that he may even have a Pulitzer Prize on his horizon someday. Hendricks definitely had a nose for the news and knew where to find it as well as write about it.

A few days before the disappearance of Linda Weigand aboard the Mardi Gras, Bill Wright had decided there might be a story in the cruise industry worth writing about, particularly with the pending bankruptcy of the Mariner cruise line. And no one seemed better suited to cover the story than Ken Hendricks.

"I want you to look into the cruise ship industry," Wright said as he sailed by Hendricks's desk on his way into his own office. "Come on in. Let's talk."

Hendricks followed Wright into his glass paneled office and sat down in the roomy guest chair opposite the publisher's desk.

"Close that damn door," Wright bellowed. "I don't want anybody else to hear what I have to say to you." Hendricks meekly complied, not knowing what was coming next. Wright was a very volatile man and any little thing could set him off sometimes.

"Look, you've seen all these problems that have been turning up on cruise ships?"

"Sure, you can't miss them. They seem to be on the news every night. If it's not a fire, it's a drowning. Some poor slob falls overboard in a drunken stupor or is pushed by his lovely new wife."

"Yeah, yeah. Exactly. I think there's something fishy going on these damn ships. I want you to look into it and see what you come up with."

"What do you mean 'fishy', these incidents all seem to be unrelated? Maybe just bad luck."

Wright clapped his hands and said, "You've got it. I like that phrase you just used: 'seem to be unrelated.' That's what I want you to find out. Are they really unrelated? I've heard some rumors that some foreign group may be behind some of these incidents. I want you to find out if that is true. This could be our biggest story yet, believe me."

"You got to be kidding" Hendricks responded.

"No, I'm definitely not kidding. There have been rumors floating around down at my yacht club that something is going on that may involve a big shake-up in the cruise industry. You know, of course, that the Mariner line is in bankruptcy. I hear that may not be an accident; that it is all part of some sort of plan that could turn the cruise industry on its head. You know how huge the cruise industry is in this area. I doubt Miami could survive without it. Any changes in that industry are gonna have a major impact on the economy. I want you to find out exactly what is happening. You know, who's behind this and what's going on."

"So, should I focus on Mariner?" Hendricks asked.

"Yeah, sure. That's as good a place to start as any. "

"By the way, who is that you are hearing this information from?"

"You know a guy named Joe Hugo? Sure you do. I saw him at the club a week or so ago and he says something is going on in the cruise industry. He said he might get involved in it himself."

Hendricks knew that Hugo was a wealthy car dealer. Like everyone else in South Florida, he had seen those crazy commercials on television. He had no idea he was a member of the publisher's yacht club. It sure didn't seem like a yacht club would be his style.

"All right, now, get outta here and get me a story."

With that, Wright picked up his cell phone and started dialing. Hendricks knew it was time to leave. "Oh, one more thing," Wright said before he left. "Another buddy of mine from the yacht club also may know something about this whole thing. His name is Bud Gorley. He's a lawyer around town. Good guy. You'll like him. You probably should to talk to him."

Hendricks began his research by pulling the clippings on line from the major newspapers detailing the various recent fires, drowning, etc. aboard cruise ships during the last year. He printed out several hundred pages and began reading them at his desk in the small, cramped newsroom. It didn't take him long to figure out a pattern. Of the six major incidents involving fires and drownings over the last year, five of them took place on Mariner ships. That seemed rather unusual to him and he wondered if anyone else was aware of this high percentage of incidents on Mariner ships. He did a little more checking and discovered that prior to last year, Mariner had never had a single such incident. Bill Wright was right: something was starting to smell "fishy."

18

Hendricks decided to follow Wright's advice as to whom he should interview. First, he called Joe Hugo's dealership to see if he could talk with him about his interest in the cruise line business. When he asked to talk to Hugo, he was told by Hugo's secretary that Mr. Hugo was leaving shortly on a cruise and wouldn't be back in the dealership for a week.

"What cruise ship is he going on?" Hendricks asked Hugo's secretary, not really expecting her to answer him.

"Why, the Mardi Gras, of course, that's his favorite ship."

Hendricks thanked the secretary and wondered if maybe he should be on that cruise also.

Before going on the cruise, Hendricks wanted to follow up with Gorley, to see what information he might have that might be useful. Hendricks, of course, knew Gorley by reputation as one of the top trial lawyers in South Florida. He had checked the court records and learned that Gorley was representing two women who claimed they had been raped aboard the Mardi Gras. Hendricks went to Gorley's office in downtown Miami. It was very impressive. On the door to his office suite, the name of the firm was emblazoned in gold leaf, "R. Stirling Gorley & Associates." The offices looked like they had been newly remodeled, with lots of light flooding the reception area from the floor to ceiling windows.

"My name is Ken Hendricks," he told the receptionist at the entrance to the office. "I'm a reporter for the Miami Tribune-Gazette and I was wondering if Mr. Gorley had some time to speak to me."

"May I tell him why you wish to speak to him, Mr. Hendricks?"

"Just say that his friend, Bill Wright, suggested I talk to him."

"Of course," said the receptionist. "Please have a seat. I'll tell him you are here."

Hendricks sat down on one of the brown leather couches that made up the reception area. He picked up a copy of the firm brochure that was sitting on the coffee table and stuffed it in his pocket. He thought to himself, you never know what you might find in one of those brochures.

Shortly after he had sat down, Gorley came out of his office. "Mr. Hendricks, I'm Bud Gorley. I'm pleased to meet you. Please come into my office."

Hendricks was impressed that Gorley had come out himself to greet him and followed him into his office.

"Mr. Gorley," Hendricks began.

"Please call me Bud."

"Okay, Bud, my editor, Bill Wright suggested I came to see you." Before Hendricks could go any further, Gorley jumped in.

"Bill's a wonderful fella. I see him very often at the yacht club. His boat is in a slip near mine. We get along real well."

"That's nice," responded Hendricks, not knowing what else to say.

"Are you writing about the club or yachting? Is that why Bill asked you to come and see me? I know quite a bit about both. You see, I was president of the yacht club for several years and I made it a point to study its history. I have a whole file filled with information on the club."

"No, Bud, that's not why I am here," said Hendricks.

Gorley was visibly disappointed. "Then why are you here? Is it about my boat? I just had it refurbished."

"No," Hendricks answered him. "It's about the Mariner cruise line. Mr. Wright suggested to me that you might know something about the problems that Mariner has faced recently, including its bankruptcy."

As soon as Hendricks mentioned Mariner, Gorley turned away and shook his head.

"I'm afraid Bill is all wrong about that. I know nothing about Mariner. And if you will please excuse me, I have another appointment."

With that, Gorley got up from his desk and escorted Hendricks out of his office.

"Say 'hello' to Bill for me," Gorley said as he began closing his office door behind him.

Hendricks thought, "I'm definitely onto something here. Something that they want to keep quiet. But who and why?"

Before Hendricks left the office, he said, "Mr. Gorley, one more thing. I understood that you had filed suit against Mariner in connection with a rape."

"Oh, that's all over with," said Gorley. "To tell you the truth, I forgot all about it."

That afternoon, Hendricks bought a ticket on the Mardi Gras cruise ship for its weekly milk run to Key West and Cozumel, Mexico. The ticket was for the cruise leaving the next day and it only cost him $198 for an inside cabin.

After Hendricks had left Gorley's office, Gorley picked up the phone and dialed Yao Lin's phone number. The phone rang and rang, but no one answered the phone. There wasn't even a voicemail box to leave a message.

"Shit," Gorley said as he finally hung up the phone. "Double shit."

19

Before I met with Hendricks, I first wanted to talk to my security guard, Roman, who had awakened me early that morning, a morning that now seemed like ages ago. I called him into my office.

"Roman," I began. "When you came to my door earlier this morning with the news about the Weigand disappearance, was there anyone else in the hall besides you, Sergeant Boudreaux, Dragan and Captain Vivaldi?"

Roman thought for a moment and then answered, "No, I don't think so."

"Think back," I said. "You don't remember any of the other cabin doors opening and someone stepping into the hall as you were knocking on my door trying to wake me up?"

"No, Lieutenant. The more I think about it, the more that I am sure there was no one else in the hall and none of the doors were opened while we were there trying to wake you up."

It was as I expected. The young lady, Sun Li, could not have overheard Roman or anyone else say anything about a murder, as she had claimed when I spoke with her this morning in the dining room. That made me suspect that she knew a lot more about the disappearance of Mrs. Weigand than she was telling me. And she specifically referred to her disappearance as a murder, which was all the more troubling to me. If she was involved, I could not understand how anyone could be so brazen as to talk to me directly about the murder unless they thought they could get away with it. The thought crossed my mind that maybe they already had done so.

20

I knocked on the door of stateroom 407, the cabin where Ken Hendricks said he was staying. A tall thin man opened the door. He had short, sandy brown hair and large round glasses, which were slightly tinted in an amber color. The glasses gave his face a strangely angelic glow. He was dressed in jeans and a blue tee shirt with a large red Nike Swoosh on the front of it. He looked like a college kid who I had awakened from a nap.

"I'm Lieutenant Morales," I said as I stepped into the small, interior, windowless cabin.

"I guess your newspaper is not very success-ful if this is the best cabin they can afford to put you in," I said.

Hendricks laughed and asked me to sit down. The only spot available was on the single bed because he had his other clothes draped over the one chair in the cabin.

"Lieutenant," he began, "thanks for coming. I take it you were intrigued by my note?"

I just nodded and he continued, "Well, since I came on board the cruise ship a few days ago, I have spoken to a number of the crew members about the various, shall I say, 'troubles' that have occurred on board the ship in the last year or so. They were almost unanimous in saying they felt some of these and maybe all of these so-called inci-dents were caused intentionally."

I was miffed that this reporter had been speaking to the crew without my permission, but, I definitely was very interested in hearing what he had found out from the crew about these incidents. These incidents had also bothered me since I had come on board the ship.

"What did the crew tell you about the reasons that these incidents were, as you say, intentionally brought about?"

"The consensus among the crew members that I talked with was that someone was deliberately trying to sabotage this ship and the other Mariner ships in order to make the cruise line less valuable. You know, of course, that Mariner already is in bankruptcy. Some of them believe that the buyer could then pluck the company out of bankruptcy at a cheap price. Also, they were afraid for their own lives. Nobody wants to die in a fire on a ship or some other such incident."

I thought for a moment and then asked him directly, "Who do you think is behind all of these incidents?"

"That's what I can't figure out yet, but I thought you might be able to help me with my story. My boss is after me to write a story exposing these problems. Do you have any idea as to who might benefit from a downturn in the fortunes of the cruise line?"

"Even if I did," I replied, "why would I tell you?"

"Why not? If you can give me some idea who might be behind this, if you know, you may be the hero who saved the cruise line. Or at least, I can write it that way."

"Sorry," I said as I stood up. "I have no desire to be the 'hero', as you say." I then headed towards the door.

Before I could get the door open, Hendricks said, "What about the murder last night on the ship?"

"I don't know what you are talking about," I lied. "I will say that we are looking for a passenger, who has somehow slipped through our fingers. But I am sure she will eventually turn up. There has been no evidence of a murder aboard this ship," I said as I left Hendricks' cabin. "Nothing like that at all."

It was now midafternoon and my theory that Mrs. Weigand had shacked up with someone other than her husband was now out the window. Obviously, the only other rational prospect was that in fact she was dead. But murder, no, there was no evidence of that yet in my mind.

I thought Hendricks was a nice enough fellow—for a reporter, but I wasn't sure I could really trust him. I'll need to figure out a way to keep him at bay and certainly keep him from any more discussions with the crew.

21

As soon as Morales left Hendricks' cabin, Hendricks was on his cell phone to his editor.

"Hello, this is Bill Wright."

"This is Hendricks, Mr. Wright."

"You still on that damn boat? You got anything for me? I have a paper to get out in a few days," Wright bellowed into the phone. Hendricks thought Wright was his usual charming self. "I'd like to have something from you in the paper about this whole cruise line thing. My own sources back here are telling me that something is going down on one of the Mariner ships right now. They seemed to think it might be something big. What do you have for me?"

"Yeah, it may be something big."

"So, tell me about it. You know how I hate suspense, goddam it," Wright said, even more impatiently than usual.

"Well, I'm on the Mariner ship, the Mardi Gras, and it seems like there may have been a murder on the ship."

"Murder? Tell me more."

"There is a rumor that a woman on her honeymoon was murdered last night on the ship. Or at least she is missing since no one has been able to find her so far."

"Hell, which is it? Is she dead or just invisible? As far as I am concerned, the better story is probably that she is missing since we can write it up for multiple days' papers. And you say this is just a rumor? We can't publish rumors like the National Enquirer. We need facts, not rumors."

"Well, that's what I'm trying to get you, the facts. I just spoke to Lieutenant Morales, the head of security on the Mardi Gras, and he denies that there has been a murder on board so maybe you'll get your wish."

"Jimminy Christmas, Hendricks, you had better find out what's going on there pretty damn soon. I would love to get this in this week's paper but I can't hold the paper forever."

"Can you do me a favor?" asked Hendricks.

"What the hell do you want? You're the reporter. I shouldn't be doing your damn legwork."

"I understand, but I'm here on the ship and I need some information that maybe you or one of the other reporters can dig up for me."

"Whaddya need?"

"I'd like to have someone look into this guy, Mario Morales, the head of security aboard the Mardi Gras."

"Why?"

"I just have a feeling."

"All right, done. I trust your feelings. You really came through on that Miami corruption thing, so I gotta trust you now on this. But you had better get back to me soon on this murder thing. This could be big, especially if we are the first paper to break the story. Hot damn that would be good."

With that, Wright hung up the phone.

22

Wright called Hendricks back about an hour later.

"Hendricks," he began. "Your buddy, Morales, he ain't exactly what he seems."

"What do you mean?"

"I called one of my buddies on the LAPD, where he had worked for some twenty years or so before retiring."

"Oh, yeah, how'd you find that out?"

"You know a good reporter never reveals his sources. Anyways, seems like he's boosted his rank."

"What do you mean?" asked Hendricks.

"Well, seems like he had been a Lieutenant but got busted down to Sergeant for some screw up."

"Is that it? So, he gave himself a promotion when he joined the Mariner cruise line. Doesn't seem to me to be that big of a deal, does it?"

"There's more to it than that. He apparently had a breakdown a couple of years ago when he was working for the LAPD. Some screw up, some sort of botched investigation. I don't know all the details. Maybe you can find out."

"Wow," said Hendricks.

"Yeah, he might be a good story himself. Give some thought to it. You know, human interest kind of thing, Could be a good sidebar to the main story on the ships' problems."

"All right, I'll talk to Morales about it and see what I can come up with."

"You gotta do better than that. I want a story and a damn good one," said Wright.

With that, Wright hung up the phone.

23

When the ship docked at the Port of Miami the next day, the Miami/Dade police and the FBI were waiting on the shore for the Mardi Gras. Of course I was aware that Sergeant Boudreaux had previously advised both agencies of the disappearance of Mrs. Weigand. But I made sure that I would be the one to greet them as they came aboard the ship.

"I'm Special Agent Philip Benson of the FBI," said the tall, athletic man in a gray suit as he reached out to shake my hand.

"I'm Lieutenant Mario Morales," I said

"Nice to meet you, Lieutenant. This is Sergeant Howard Duffy of the Miami/Dade police department."

"I think we've met before, Sergeant Duffy," I said as I nodded in the direction of Duffy.

"I don't think so," replied Duffy as he turned away abruptly.

I was certain that Duffy had been involved in a matter several years ago when I was still with the LAPD. I recalled that Duffy had been working homicide in another section of LA. I was appointed to the police review board regarding an interrogation of a Hispanic boy by Duffy in connection with a murder investigation. The boy confessed to the murder but before trial, his lawyer claimed that the confession was coerced. The judge agreed and threw out the confession. Since there was no other evidence the boy was released. Later on, the real killer was found and charged with the murder. The

Hispanic boy's lawyer filed charges with the Police Review board. The other members of the board found that Duffy had not exceeded the proper bounds of interrogation, but I dissented from the decision. I could not believe that the other members of the board went against the Judge's ruling. No wonder Duffy preferred not to acknowledge my existence.

"Now that the ship is in dock," Benson began, "we will take over the investigation of the Weigand matter, Lieutenant. I have a search warrant from Federal Court signed by Judge McFarland. We will begin the search of the entire ship. I have a whole team of agents waiting to come aboard. And, Lieutenant, could you please give me your file?"

"I don't have a file, per se," I replied. "I prefer to keep everything in my head when doing an investigation."

"No file? Well, that's not very helpful," said Benson.

"I have a file," said Sergeant Boudreaux, who appeared suddenly from behind me, seemingly from nowhere.

"Who are you?" asked Benson.

"I'm Sergeant Virginia Boudreaux," she said. "I'm the deputy head of security aboard the Mardi Gras. I was the one who contacted your office."

I looked at her sharply but said nothing. She knew that I hated nothing more than someone not going through channels. I knew nothing about this file she was referring to. And now she was handing it over to the FBI when I had never seen it.

"Yes, yes, I recall your call. So, what does the file show?" asked Benson.

"The primary thing in the file is a video from one of the ship's surveillance cameras that shows a rather large man tossing what appears to be a black trash bag overboard at 3 a.m. on the night of the disappearance of Mrs. Weigand. There are also some other videos that might be helpful that show Mrs. Weigand and another person the night of her disappearance."

"Interesting," said Benson. "Any idea who it might be in the video throwing the black bag overboard?"

"Maybe. I do have some idea who it is, but the picture is quite blurry due to the poor lighting."

"You know we have all kinds of enhancement techniques available. If we use those, it might become a little clearer," said Benson.

"Well, thank you Sergeant Boudreaux. That should be very helpful. Please join us later back at our office in the Federal Building," said Benson. Benson did not extend a similar invitation to me.

With that, Boudreaux, Benson and Duffy brushed past me and onto the ship. I was left behind, nursing my hurt feelings.

By then the passengers had begun disembarking down the gangway. Out of the corner of my eye, I thought that I spotted the elusive Sun Li. She was with what looked like three other Chinese men. I hurried down the gangplank after them, pushing my way through a crowd of disembarking passengers. By the time I was able to get to the bottom, the woman and the others were gone. I did see a long, black stretch limo pull away from the curb with screeching tires as it left the dock area. The windows were darkened so I could not be sure who was in there. But, in any event, it appeared to me that someone was clearly in a great hurry to get away from the ship.

24

I kept a small apartment in Little Havana on SW 4th street, near Jose Marti Park. It was a one bedroom with a small kitchenette. For $1200 a month, it was pretty small. But it was clean and I liked the building and the other tenants who lived there, mostly Hispanics, like me. The living room area was sparsely furnished with a couch, love seat and a 19 inch television I had brought out from LA in the VW bus when I drove across the country from California to Miami. I had bought a bed and nightstand in Miami as well as a small rocking chair, where I would sometimes sit and smoke one of my few remaining Montecristo cigars.

After I retired from the LAPD, I had to decide what I would do with the rest of my life. One thing I knew was that I wanted to travel. I had always wanted to see the country, so I bought an old Volkswagen camper, with a hundred and twenty-five thousand miles on it that I was lucky enough to find in pretty good shape. I just took off headed East along Route 66 or at least what was left of it. It took me almost nine months to travel across America, stopping at campgrounds and Wal-Mart parking lots. You would be amazed at the people you meet on the road. They say that people who run away are running towards something. Don't believe that for a minute. The people I met were all running from something. Including me.

Somehow, I'm not even sure how or why, after those nine months on the road, I found myself in Miami, Florida. I had driven over 17,000 miles in the old Volkswagen and it was just about shot. It seemed as good a place to stop as any.

I sold the camper for next to nothing to a used car dealer and rented the apartment in Little Havana. I soon felt right at home there.

Because I spoke Spanish reasonably well, I became quite friendly with a number of retired Cuban men who lived in apartments in my building or in nearby buildings. Every morning I would meet a group of them at a small coffee shop located on Calle Ocho, the main street in Little Havana. I would sit and eat buttery, thick Cuban toast. I would then wash it down with a thick, creamy Cuban coffee called café con leche. It would go down smooth as silk. As we were eating and drinking, I would listen to their stories about how wonderful Cuba had been before Fidel. They all proclaimed their desire to return to Cuba someday if he were gone. But I really wondered if they would ever go back even if they had the chance. Their children and grandchildren were all born in the United States and were Americans. What did they really have to go back to anyways?

Later in the morning, a group of us would adjourn to nearby Domino Park and play dominoes or chess until lunch. I surprised myself and became quite good at chess, a game I had never really played before.

After six months of drinking that strong coffee and sitting in the sun in the park playing chess, I realized that I was becoming bored out of my mind. I began to think that maybe I had retired too soon. I had loved being a cop despite some problems I had encountered near the end of my career. I knew I was too good a cop at heart to sit around all day drinking coffee and playing chess or an odd game of dominoes.

Fortunately, through a friend of mine I got an interview for a job as head of security aboard the Mardi Gras. It didn't pay a lot, but it supplemented my pension from the LAPD. And there were the extra perks of free room and board on the ship.

The ship was to be in dock for a few days so my apartment was where I would spend my off-duty time, mostly sleeping or reading, I thought. Now that the Weigand matter was out of my hands, I had little to do.

So, I climbed into bed. And even though it was only 11 a.m., I fell asleep immediately.

The next morning at 6 a.m., my cell phone rang. I woke up at the sound of the crashing cymbals I used as my ring tone.

"Hello," I gasped into the phone in a barely coherent voice. I was still half asleep even though I had slept some 18 hours or so. That much sleep always made me feel groggy. I also had a pounding headache.

"You had better turn your television on," came the voice at the other end of the phone line.

I recognized the voice as belonging to Doc Philips, the ship's doctor and the one person on the ship I felt I could trust.

"Why?" I managed to mumble.

"Turn it on. You'll see," said the doctor. "You'll see", he repeated and hung up the phone.

I did as I was told. I stumbled out of bed and turned on the television. I flipped through the channels, which, at that hour, were mostly filled with infomercials touting exercise equipment that was expensive and impossible to understand how to use or herbs that promised sexual prowess beyond human belief. Finally, I came across a news channel. It seemed like some sort of news conference was going on as the words "Breaking News" flashed across the screen.

I stood up quickly when I saw that on the podium were Special Agent Benson, Sergeant Duffy and Sergeant Boudreaux. I turned up the volume of the television as high as I could.

Special Agent Benson was just beginning to speak:

"My name is Special Agent Benson. I am with the Miami office of the FBI and I am here to announce that we have solved the mystery of the disappearance of Mrs. Linda Weigand from the cruise ship Mardi Gras during a cruise from Cozumel, Mexico earlier this week. We have in custody a man who we believe to be the person responsible for her disappearance and apparent death. His name is Joseph Vaughn Hugo, age 56, from Miami, Florida."

Just then a booking picture of Joe Hugo flashed on the screen followed by a short video of Hugo. He was wearing an orange jump suit. Both his hands and feet were shackled as he shuffled, head down from a police car into what looked like the local courthouse. This was the famous "perp walk" so despised by those who have been arrested, but loved by the police and news media.

Benson went on: "We think this was a classic case of a love triangle gone bad." Obviously, Benson had been talking to Sergeant Boudreaux. And like a lot of cops, he bought into the first story that seemed to make even a little sense to him. "We have a video that we believe shows the actor throwing Mrs. Weigand's body overboard," said Benson.

I turned off the television. I had heard enough. I was furious, but this whole matter was now out of my hands. I dressed and went outside to the warm air. The day was still awakening and a thick fog enveloped the city. Just like that night on the ship when Mrs. Weigand disappeared, I thought. Oh, hell, I said to myself as I walked into a small café and ordered a large, strong Cuban coffee. Life goes on.

25

The news media had a field day with this story. One newspaper headline read, "Big Auto Kahuna Caught in Sex-Murder Net." Several of the newspaper reporters had done some digging and found out that twenty years before, Hugo had once served time in a federal prison in Pennsylvania for money laundering. This arrest was what had apparently fed the persistent rumor that Hugo's success was backed by mob money.

I read these stories with interest. Certainly, I had no reason to like Hugo but I also did not think he would resort to murder. He just had too much to lose. On the other hand, being a cop myself for all those years, I knew the police mentality. As soon as some cops think they have the right person, they exclude every other possible suspect and go down that narrow path to convict the initial suspect. I had seen it hundreds of times before. It looked like the FBI and the Miami/Dade police were going down that same narrow path. And who was pushing them: I believed it was my own deputy, Sergeant Boudreaux.

In a strange way, I actually sort of felt sorry for Hugo. I knew the difficulty Hugo would have proving that he was innocent. And that was really what he would have to do. At trial, the Judge would charge the jury that he was presumed innocent and that the District Attorney must prove him guilty beyond a reasonable doubt, blah, blah, blah. But the reality, I knew, was that once you are seated in that defendant's chair at trial, you must prove your innocence, not always an easy proposition, even for an innocent man.

Well, that's somebody else's problem now, I thought. I finished my coffee and strolled over to Domino Park on Calle Ocho. It was only 7:30, but already several domino and chess games were going on. These old Cubans loved to get going early. I asked if I could join in one of the games.

"Si," said an old man in a red sweater vest and dark brown fedora as he hunched over the domino board. I sat down opposite him and spent the rest of the morning there, playing dominoes.

26

Later that same day, I was in my apartment fixing dinner. I usually just stuffed a box of something in the microwave and when the buzzer rang, I grabbed the food and ate it standing up in the kitchen. Today, though, I felt I needed something more substantial. I had gone to the Publix supermarket and I bought a thick sirloin strip steak, a baking potato and a quart of Cherry Garcia ice cream, my favorite. As I was turning the steak over in the skillet on the burner of the gas stove, I heard a knock on my door. Very odd, since no one ever came to my apartment.

"Who is it?"

"Ken Hendricks. I'd like to talk to you."

Oh shit, I thought. Just what I need right now. I wondered how he was able to find me. I guess he must be a good reporter after all.

"Go away. I have nothing to say to the press about the Hugo case. Anyways, it's no longer my case," I said through the closed door.

"I'm not here to talk to you about the Hugo case. I'm here to talk about you."

What the hell? What is he talking about?

"Go away." I yelled. "I told you I have nothing to say."

"Look," came the reply, "I want to talk to you about how you have been able to overcome your PTSD and drug problems."

I decided that I had better let him in. The last thing I needed was to have my neighbors hear about those matters.

"Come in," I said to Hendricks as I showed him to my kitchen table, where we both sat down.

"Look, Lieutenant, I'm sure that these subjects are not the type of thing you like to talk about, but my boss insisted that I discuss these matters with you. He seems to think that there might be a story there. A real human interest story."

"Your boss must have very good connections," I said as I poured a glass of water for myself.

"Let's just say that he knows a lot of people," Hendricks responded.

I had to make a quick decision as to whether to cooperate with Hendricks or let him write whatever story he could come up with on his own. I decided I would tell Hendricks the whole story so that maybe I could get my side of the story out first. The only other person I had confided in about what had happened to me was Doc Phillips.

"What would you like to know?" I finally said to Hendricks after a brief pause.

"Well," Hendricks began, "I understand that a few years back while you were working for the LAPD you suffered some sort of breakdown, maybe post-traumatic stress disorder or something like that, as a result of some murder case. Am I right there?"

"That would be the Hinchley case," I said after some hesitation. I guessed it was either now or never.

I then proceeded to explain what had happened.

"Thomas Hinchley was a notorious serial

killer, who had murdered and beheaded a string of prostitutes in the Los Angeles suburbs. You may remember him." Hendricks nodded his head.

"I had been assigned to the investigation. Early on, Hinchley's name surfaced as a possible suspect. I had interviewed Hinchley because he met the profile established by the FBI profiler. But I had to let him go because I felt there was not enough evidence to keep him in jail.

"Hinchley went on to kill five more women after I had him released. Eventually, Hinchley shot himself after a shootout with police. Hinchley killed three police officers in that shootout. I'm sure you can understand that I blamed myself for all eight of those deaths. Some other people did also because I started getting death threats in the mail. When that all happened, I started getting these excruciating headaches that just wouldn't go away. If that wasn't bad enough, I had this anxious feeling I just couldn't shake.. Some days, I could hardly get out of bed. I even thought about killing mself. That was when my wife and I started arguing all the time. It was the beginning of the end of our marriage.

"The Hinchley case was the last homicide investigation I had handled with the LAPD. When this all came down, I was reassigned to the robbery division. I thought at the time that the higher ups in the chain of command saw that I could no longer handle the stress of working homicide. I learned later that my wife had gone to the Division Commander and begged him to take me off homicide. Shortly after that we got divorced. I know now she was trying to help me, but for a long time, I was just bitter."

I told Hendricks that until I was diagnosed with PTSD, I didn't even know that under some circumstances, just about anyone could get it. I had thought it was only something that soldiers got, like the guys returning from Iraq and Afghanistan. But I learned that unusual stresses like the Hinckley debacle could also bring it on.

"How did you deal with it?" Hendricks asked after I had finished my story.

"After a period where I just tried to handle it on my own, I asked the police physician for some Valium, which was the only thing that seemed to relieve some of the pain and anxiety I was feeling. After a while, he wouldn't give me any more prescriptions, so I started going to private physicians. You would be amazed how easy it is to get prescription drugs when you are desperate.

"Eventually," I told him, "I reached bottom when I was demoted from Lieutenant to Sergeant and given a desk job at police headquarters. That was a big blow to me," I said. "Not only financially, but also to my ego. I loved being called 'Lieutenant.' I know it sounds sort of silly, but it was important to me. I was one of the first Hispanics on the force to be promoted to that rank. For that reason, I also didn't want to let my brothers down."

Hendricks was writing down everything I told him. I felt somehow like I was in confession. And believe it or not, it felt good, like I was purging myself of all my sins.

"Is that why you decided to call yourself, 'Lieutenant' when you became head of security on the Mardi Gras?"

"Of course," I said. "It did no one any harm and it makes me feel good to hear being called that again."

"How did you overcome the PTSD and the addiction to Valium?" Hendricks asked.

"Believe it or not, I began to pray a lot and I read a lot about spiritual things. I know that this sounds really corny, but in my case this approach worked. I had always been particularly interested in the Trappist monks. There was a Trappist monastery near my home in Salinas where I grew up. Even after I became a cop, I would sometimes visit the monastery for a retreat over a weekend.

I continued, "I had become quite friendly with the abbot at the Monastery. It was he who directed me to the writings of a couple of monks who were pretty famous for trying to merge Eastern and Western views on prayer and contemplation. Maybe you've heard of them, Thomas Merton and Thomas Keating?" Hendricks nodded his head.

"They both seemed totally engaged in the world despite being Trappists. I read several of Merton's works on contemplation and his autobiography, "The Seven Storey Mountain." The approach they take is sort of like this whole idea of mindfulness/meditation that you have probably read about. These days it seems like you can hardly pick up a newspaper or magazine without hearing about it.. You concentrate on the moment by focusing on your breathe. The key is to exclude all other thoughts, good and bad. You just let them wash away. I did that for several hours a day for weeks.

I'm not exactly sure how it works, but it brought me back to reality. I realized I no longer needed the crutch of the drugs I was taking. I still try to meditate every day to keep my mind clear. To me now, it's the only way to live."

"Interesting story, Lieutenant, very interesting," Hendricks said.

"Are you going to write an article about all this?"

"I'm not sure just yet, what I'm gonna do. I'm just not sure. I guess it all depends."

I didn't ask him what it depended upon but I did say, "I would rather you didn't."

27

The next day, I received a letter from the Mariner cruise line. It read in its entirety:

"As you may know, the Mariner Cruise Line is in bankruptcy. Thank you for your service to the Mariner aboard the cruise ship, the Mardi Gras. Your services, however, are no longer needed. A check for your remaining compensation is enclosed. Best of luck in the future."

The letter was stamped with the name "L. Lewis", director of human relations. Not even a real person had signed the check or the letter. The enclosed check was for the sum of $825.39. Included with the check was a list of deductions. These included $48 for my 401k plan. I laughed when I saw that. It was highly unlikely that I would be contributing any more to that plan.

In some strange way, I felt a sense of relief. The stress of the job and particularly this Weigand matter had been taking a toll on my health. I could see it happening and I had felt it also. So, maybe this is a good thing, I thought. I can wash my hands of the matter and get a new job, maybe working in a café or something where the stress levels are a lot less. I had been fooling myself, I thought, that I could just go back into police work without any adverse consequences. I was wrong. There are always consequences. Always.

28

A few days after I had been fired, I was sitting in my apartment smoking my last Montecristo cigar when the phone rang.

"Hello," I answered.

"May I please speak to Lieutenant Mario Morales?"

I did not recognize the voice at the other end, but it was quite compelling in its tone.

"This is Morales. Who is calling?"

".My name is Bud Gorley. I'm so glad you are there and that I was able to reach you. I hope you are not too busy to speak to me."

I recognized the name immediately, of course. But I could not imagine why Gorley would be calling me. At first, I thought maybe he had heard I had been fired and he was soliciting my business for a lawsuit against the cruise line for age discrimination or maybe race discrimination because I was Hispanic. I had actually been thinking about looking into that possibility myself. Or maybe he was calling about that deposition in the rape case that was scheduled in just a few days. In any event, I had no idea why he was calling or what was in the offing.

"Lieutenant Morales," Gorley said, "it has not been widely-publicized yet, but I have been retained to represent Joe Hugo in connection with this Weigand matter."

So that was it. I should have figured that out myself. I knew about Gorley's reputation and knew that Hugo needed the best lawyer he could get. But why is Gorley calling me? What can I do for him?

"As you might expect, Mr. Hugo has public-ly proclaimed his innocence and privately he has told me the same thing, which was that he had noth-ing to do with the disappearance of Mrs. Weigand. I believe him. I don't know what your feeling is re-garding his guilt or innocence, Lieutenant, but I would like to talk to you about your investigation of this matter. I know you may have certain ethical obligations that you owe to the Mariner Company. And you can be sure that I am not now and never would ask you to violate those obligations. But it would be helpful to me, and, of course, Mr. Hugo, to get your perspective on this matter now that you are no longer employed by the Mariner cruise line."

I was quite surprised at this turn of events. This certainly was not something I had anticipated. I also was a little puzzled as to how Gorley knew I had been fired. I wondered what exactly Gorley meant when he referred to my "perspective" on the Weigand disappearance. Yet, I had to admit, Gorley sounded very persuasive. I understood now how he could sway a jury in his client's favor even in the most egregious case.

"Thank you, Mr. Gorley. I obviously need to think about it before I can give you an answer," I said. "You have got to admit, this is a very unusual offer. I'm not really sure I can help you much in any event, but I will give some thought to your offer and will get back to you as soon as I have the opportuni-ty to mull it over and decide what to do. I will say that it is a very intriguing offer."

122 · AJ BASINSKI

"I understand completely," responded Gorley. "I understand. You can reach me anytime on my cell phone at 888-123-4567. I will wait to hear from you, Lieutenant, and I hope it will be with an affirmative response to my request. Oh, by the way, you need not concern yourself about that negligence suit I brought on behalf of the two girls who were alleging they had been raped by one of the crew members aboard the Mardi Gras. I settled that case recently with the cruise line's insurance carrier. It wasn't much of a case to begin with. But we did reach an amicable settlement and my clients are pleased. I am telling you this because if you were concerned

that you would be deposed in connection with that case, you needn't worry any more. It's all taken care of. The case has been dismissed. I will wait to hear from you, Lieutenant. Goodbye."

I hung up the phone. I had to admit that I was impressed by Gorley. He clearly knew what he was doing. But I was struck by Gorley's view of the rape case and the decision to settle it so quickly. Gorley seemed almost cavalier about that case. I was surprised that he was settling the case for what probably was a relatively small amount of money. I knew that the cruise line's insurance carrier had taken a hard line on this case so I doubt that they had coughed up the kind of six and seven figure settlements that Gorley was used to getting. The decision to settle seemed very much unlike this high-flying trial lawyer. Then again, maybe, just like me, he needed the money to tide him over for a while.

I re-lit my Montecristo, which had gone out while I was on the phone. I sat rocking on my chair as I thought about Gorley's offer. We hadn't talked money, but I assumed I would be well-paid. And anyways, I now had no income at all, at least until my unemployment compensation kicked in, which would not be for several weeks. And even then, the unemployment check would not be enough to live on in pricey Miami. My rent on the apartment was due in two weeks and I was not sure how I was going to pay it. I definitely could use the money right now.

There was one other thought that ran through my mind: the disappearance of my sister Teresa years before. She had disappeared while visiting Disneyland with the family she was working for as a nanny. I was still hoping to find her even though I knew in my heart that I would never find my sister either alive or dead. Maybe if I could find Linda Weigand or at least find out what happened to her, it might give me some comfort in a strange way that I really could not fully explain.

As I mulled over these thoughts, I watched the blue cigar smoke from my Montecristo filling the air in my room and seeping out the open transom over the door and into the hall. I hoped none of the neighbors would complain about the smell of the cigar.as it wafted through the corridors of the apartment building.

29

I called Ken Hendricks later that same day. After our meeting in my apartment, he and I had reached an agreement or understanding of sorts: he agreed that he would not write about my PTSD or addiction problems if I agreed to keep him informed about the Hugo matter. It was sort of a détente between us. Because at the time of our agreement, I didn't expect to have anything more to do with the Hugo case, I readily agreed. Obviously now, with Gorley's phone call and, particularly if I accepted his offer, that all would change. I thought I should tell Ken about the call and my decision regarding the offer, particularly in light of the pressure his boss was putting on Ken for a story. Maybe there still would be one. So I gave Ken a call at the newsroom of the Miami Tribune-Gazette.

"Hello, Ken, this is Mario."

"Hi Mario, glad to hear from you. I have sort of reached a dead end on the Hugo side of the story, but I do have something that may interest you. I also hope that you have some new information that might help me with my story."

I assured him that I was calling about the Hugo matter, but probably not for the reason he may have thought. "I just got a strange call from Bud Gorley, you know, Hugo's lawyer," I said.

"What do you mean, 'strange,'?" Ken replied.

"He wants me to work on the Hugo case with him as an investigator."

"Wow. That's kind of unusual, isn't it, since you were involved in the initial investigation of Linda Weigand's disappearance.

"I thought so too, but Gorley assured me he would not ask for any 'inside' information. Whatever that means."

"You gonna take him up on the offer?"

"I'm thinking about it." I was thinking about it quite seriously at this point. I still remembered the fear that I saw in my mother's eyes when my sister disappeared some thirty years before. I felt like I had to find Linda Weigand even though I could never find my little sister. I owed it to my sister to try.

"You know, I've done a little checking up on this Gorley guy and I found out some surprising stuff about him," said Hendricks.

"Oh yeah, like what?"

"Well, my editor's been on my back about this story and I decided to do a little digging to see what I could find. All the other papers and reporters are digging into Hugo's past and some of them are also looking into the background of the Weigands. I thought I would take a little different tack."

"And, what did you find out?"

"Gorley is not exactly what he seems. You know, he comes across in those television commercials as this really wealthy guy, without a care in the world about his financial situation. What I found out is that he is in quite a bit of debt. His house is heavily mortgaged and his wife is a big spender like you would not believe."

"So what? Is that newsworthy?"

"No, not by itself, but I heard some rumors that he has had some involvement with a Chinese businessman named Yao Lin. It seems this Yao guy is a big wig with some Shanghai company called Shanghai Blue and that company is making acquisitions in the U.S. in a big way. It's kinda scary."

"So, what is Gorley doing for them?" I asked.

"That's still not clear, but I do know this: this Yao guy and his company are rumored to be heavily involved in the drug trade in the Middle East, particularly in opium and some other new drugs."

A light went on in my head.

"What kind of new drugs?" I asked.

"Something called 'spice.' I never heard of it before, but I'm told it is some kind of synthetic marijuana that kids can buy in convenience stores. The DEA is just starting to crack down on it since there have been a rash of bad trips recently among high school students, boys in particular."

"Are you sure about this, Ken?"

"Pretty damn sure. My sources are always pretty good about stuff like that."

I knew that it would not help to ask him who his sources were, since I was sure that like most reporters, he guarded them closer than his own children.

When I heard this information, something else clicked on in my mind. When I had been hired as chief of security aboard the Mardi Gras, while I was filling out the usual employment forms, the Mariner HR person had told me that the former head of security had been fired because two of his guards had been found smuggling a large quantity of cocaine aboard the ship while in port in Cozumel. His name, I was told, was Victor Ortiz. That was the first time I had heard his name, but I had a premonition that it would not be the last. This time I was correct.

30

The next day, I called Gorley and we agreed to meet for lunch so that I could let him know what my response was to his offer of employment as an investigator on the Hugo case.

"I'm so glad you could make it," Gorley said as he extended his hand across the restaurant table to me as I sat down opposite him. It was a warm day and we sat outside on the patio of Joe's Crab Shack. Joe's was a really nice and pricey Miami restaurant that I had heard about. I had always wanted to eat there since I had arrived in Miami, but I knew that I simply couldn't afford it. This was confirmed to me when I quickly scanned the price list for the entrees and saw that everything was a la carte and quite expensive. I wasn't worried, though, because I assumed that Gorley would be picking up the tab for this lunch.

"Please feel free to order anything on the menu, Lunch is on me," Gorley confirmed. "I think you will particularly like the stone crabs. They are the specialty here. They serve it with this great mustard sauce. And should we have a little wine with our lunch? Would you care for some white?"

I nodded my head and Gorley continued.

"A nice fume blanc goes well with crab. I see they have a very nice 1998 fume. If that is all right with you, I'll order a bottle."

Without skipping a beat and before I could say a word, Gorley summoned the waiter to our table, ordered the stone crabs for both of us and then asked the sommelier to bring us a bottle of the fume blanc. I had no real idea of the price of the wine, and I assumed it was a bundle, but Gorley never asked the waiter or sommelier. I was beginning to wonder if Hendricks was really right that Gorley was in financial difficulty or maybe this was just part of his act.

I could see immediately that Gorley was very smooth in his demeanor. But I also thought that he came across as really likable. I have found that you usually can tell a lot about a person when you see how he (or she) treats the wait staff in a restaurant. Sometimes, these so-called big shots treat them like they hardly exist. I felt Gorley had treated the waiter with respect. I had seen many four flushers who thought that they were charming but, in reality, they were just slimeballs. I didn't get the impression that Gorley was like that. I could see how Gorley could easily get a jury in the palm of his hand.

"Thank you for inviting me to lunch. It is a pleasure to meet you, Mr. Gorley," I said. "I've heard a lot about you, of course. In my opinion, for what it's worth, I think Mr. Hugo made the right choice in selecting you as his counsel."

"Well, thank you, Lieutenant. I very much appreciate your confidence in me," Gorley responded.

After receiving the call from Gorley the day before, I had gone to the public library in Miami to research Gorley's background on my own. I began by checking him out in the lawyer's directory, Martindale-Hubbell. He was given the highest possible ranking, AV, which really surprised me. This meant he had the highest ranking for both legal expertise and ethics. In light of his problem in Florida a few years back concerning his solicitation of clients, I was a little surprised to see he still received the highest marks. Maybe those rankings could be bought, I wondered.

I also was surprised to learn that Gorley had written several books on the practice of law. The one that had been a best-seller was called simply, "The Art of Persuasion". I checked the book out of the library and took it back to my apartment. It was a short book and I was able to read it through in an evening. It was a quick read, but I thought Gorley made some excellent points in the book. "Being a good trial lawyer," Gorley wrote, "is nothing more than being a good story teller." That made sense to me because everyone likes a good story, including juries and judges. Even judges were human, he wrote, and they will respond to a compelling story just like anyone else.

I got the feeling that Gorley was a great story-teller and that, undoubtedly, was the key to his phenomenal success at trial. I would definitely want him on my side, I thought. Definitely. No wonder Joe Hugo decided to retain him.

"Lieutenant," began Gorley.

"Just call me Mario. I'm just plain Mario, now"

"And please call me 'Bud', everybody else does."

"OK, Bud."

"Thank you for the nice compliment. I certainly hope you are right that Joe made the right choice in selecting me as his attorney. But let me first say to you that I am truly sorry to hear about your loss. It's a shame that you were fired from your job like that. I'm sure it was quite a blow."

"It is not the first time I've been dealt a sharp blow like that," I said.

"Let me get right to the point, Mario," Gorley continued. "I need your help. I think that working together we can make a great team that can provide the best possible legal representation to Mr. Hugo. My former investigator has resigned and left town because of his wife's transfer so I was looking for a new investigator to help me with this and, perhaps, other matters as well. As I said in the phone call, I want to make one thing clear: I am not asking you to betray any confidence with the former owners of Mariner."

I interrupted him at this point, "What do you mean, 'former owners of Mariner'? I thought Mr. Hugo was going to buy Mariner out of bankruptcy? Has that taken place already?"

"He was going to buy it, but, of course, his arrest and the scandal associated with it led the judge to disqualify him from the bidding. The Mariner Line is probably going to be sold to a Chinese businessman from Shanghai. This is not public yet, but that is what has happened. Of course, the whole transaction is still subject to approval by the federal government and the bankruptcy court itself. But that is likely just a formality at this point, particularly because there are no other bidders out there with the money to make the purchase now that Hugo is out of the picture. I feel bad for Joe, of course. The Chinese government is paying a premium of 300 million dollars for the entire cruise line. In cash, of course."

I took this all in, but remained silent. Obviously, Ken Hendricks's sources were quite good.

Finally, I said, "I'll give you whatever help I can, but keep in mind, we were just at the beginning of the investigation on board the ship. There was a lot that has to be done before we can rule out anyone as a suspect in this case, including your client, Mr. Hugo."

"I certainly understand that," said Gorley. "But let me say this, I do think Hugo is innocent of this crime, if indeed there has even been a crime. We still don't have the faintest idea where Mrs. Weigand is, do we? For all we know, she may be alive and well, living somewhere in Miami."

"You are right, of course. In my experience, too often some cops jump to a conclusion early on in the investigation and do not look at all the facts that may suggest another suspect or even a different cause of death. I want you to understand that I am not like that. I believe you can only solve a crime, if you know and have studied and repeatedly analyzed all of the relevant facts."

"You and I will work well together," said Gorley with a smile on his face. "From your answer, I take it you will join the defense team for Mr. Hugo."

I shrugged my shoulders and just said, "Agreed."

"I think that it is important that I meet with

Mr. Hugo as soon as possible," I said. "Last time I spoke with him, he was very abrupt with me and refused to talk about what had happened the night of Mrs. Weigand's disappearance other than in a very general way."

Gorley responded quickly, "I agree. When I told him that I was considering retaining you to assist in the investigation, he told me about your meeting on board the ship. Hugo expressed his profound regrets to me concerning his actions. He thought it was very boorish of him .He would like to apologize to you in person, I'm sure. I will contact the warden and, unless you hear otherwise, I will meet you at the Dade County jail tomorrow morning at 9 o'clock. You can talk to Hugo then."

We then finished our meals, which were quite good, as well as the bottle of fume blanc which Gorley had ordered. I don't remember ever having drunk a wine quite as good before. After he paid the bill, Gorley said he had to leave for a court appearance. We shook hands and Gorley got up and left the table. He left behind a long white envelope with my name on it. When Gorley was out of sight, I opened it. Inside was ten thousand dollars in hundred dollar bills. I had never seen so many "Benjamins" as they were referred to on the street. Drug dealers particularly liked the "Benjamins" because it was much easier to transport the drug money that way than with smaller bills. Even a hundred thousand dollars in hundreds was a heavy load. I did wonder where Gorley got all those hundreds.

I put the envelope in my inside coat

pocket. I kept tapping it as I walked to my car, just to make sure it was still there. At least now I would be able to pay my rent.

31

The Miami-Dade County Pre-Trial Detention Center is like jails everywhere. It is over-crowded, loud, smells of urine and other nasty odors. It is not a place where you want to spend a lot time if you can avoid it. One difference from other jails is that the Miami-Dade County jail sits in the middle of this sunny and warm paradise called Miami. But none of the Florida sunshine filters into this jail to brighten the day for the prisoners, particularly those in solitary confinement where Joe Hugo was being held. The federal magistrate, at Hugo's initial arraignment held shortly after his arrest, had denied Gorley's request for bail, calling Hugo "a definite flight risk." So, it appeared likely that Hugo would have to remain in jail until trial.

Gorley and I met with Hugo in the lawyers' conference room of the jail. It was a small airless room that smelled of mildew from the concrete floor. Hugo was brought in by two burly guards with both his hands and feet shackled. One of the guards released the shackles from his hands as Hugo sat down at the conference table across from me and Gorley. I thought Hugo had already lost weight. Maybe prison food would be good for his weight problem.

"You remember Lieutenant Morales," Gorley said as he reached across the table to shake Hugo's hand.

"Sure" said Hugo. "Last time we met, I wasn't very cooperative, was I, Lieutenant?"

I nodded my head but remained quiet. His mistaking me for the steward bringing him his lunch still rankled me.

"You see," Hugo continued, "I was in the middle of this big deal to buy the cruise line and I didn't need any distractions. That's no excuse, I know, but I really would like your help."

I thought that was an odd choice of words. One of his employees is missing and maybe even dead, yet he thought of it as a mere "distraction."

"Did you have anything to do with the disappearance of Linda Weigand?" I blurted out.

"No, I know absolutely nothing about what happened to her. Nothing. Why would I want to harm her? It makes no sense. I had no reason to."

"Are you aware that the police have a video from one of the ship's surveillance cameras showing a man, who they are claiming is you, throwing a black bag overboard at 3 o'clock in the morning the day of Linda's disappearance?"

Hugo paused, and then said, "I know. I don't think it is me, but I'm not sure."

Hugo said this in a very matter of fact way. This virtual admission of possible guilt took me off guard. I had assumed that Hugo would simply deny that was him in the video, but all he can say is "I don't think it is me, but I'm not sure." Men in Florida have been executed for murder on much less evidence than that.

I bluntly told Hugo, "You know no one is going to believe that you don't remember what happened that night. There is a video of a man dumping a black bag into the water. If your testimony is that

'I don't remember,' the jury will assume that you are lying and convict you in a flash."

Hugo looked me squarely in the eye: "It happens to be true. What I need is to have you and Mr. Gorley here, prove is that I had nothing to do with Linda's disappearance or murder or whatever. Because I didn't. I swear I didn't."

I pointed out to Hugo that if he didn't remember, how could he say he didn't do it? I think that caught him by surprise.

I decided to try a different tack with Hugo. "I understand that you were seen playing blackjack with Mrs. Weigand the night of her disappearance," I said, trying to shift the focus of our discussion.

Hugo looked a little startled when I said this, as though he was thinking "how does he know all this about me."

"I might have. It wouldn't surprise me. I love to play blackjack and she might have been at the same table with me. I don't know."

Gorley then stepped in and said, "Have you spoken to anyone else about what happened that night?"

"Yeah, well, when I was first arrested, they took me to the station house and put me in this little room. A couple of cops came in and asked me some questions."

"What did you tell them?" I asked.

"Well, I'm not sure exactly. But I know I didn't do anything to Linda, I can tell you that."

"Did you try to have sex with Linda that night back in your suite after you left the casino?"

"I dunno, I might have," Hugo responded as

he put his head down on the table on top of his crossed arms.

"What do you mean that you 'might have' tried to have sex with Linda that night? Either you did try or you didn't, what is it? No more games." I was getting disgusted with this guy now.

"I just don't remember. I don't remember."

Was this a case of convenient amnesia, I asked myself. I had seen it before in several homicide investigations I had conducted while I was still with LAPD. Sometimes it is real because the enormity of what the individual had done simply does not register. Was that what happened here? I had to find out.

I knew what he had told Boudreaux about the noise he claimed to have heard coming from the Weigand stateroom next door to his, so I decided to ask him about that as well.

"I understand that you told my deputy that you heard a noise that night coming from the Weigand suite next door to yours. Is that true and what type of noise was it?"

Hugo put his head down on his crossed arms on the conference table and said, "I think I did, but I'm really not sure. She kept pestering me, like she thought I was responsible for Linda's disappearance. So I embellished the story to make it seem like I was sure. I know it was stupid, but it seemed like a good idea at the time to get the heat off my back."

"Did you tell that same story to any of the police or FBI agents who interviewed you after you were arrested?"

"I don't think so, but I'm not really sure. I just can't remember everything I told them. I wish I could. I wish I could."

With that little exchange, Gorley and I left Mr. Hugo, who was being taken back to his cell.

"I didn't do it. I really didn't," Hugo shouted as one of the guards closed the door to the conference room.

32

"What do you think of our client, Mr. Hugo?" Gorley asked me as we walked to our cars in the jail parking lot.

I waited a moment before responding and then decided to deflect the question rather than answer him directly. "Do you believe him? That he can't really remember what happened that night" I asked Gorley.

I could see Gorley was a little taken aback by my question but he answered: "You know what, I actually do. But proving his innocence in a court of law is not going to be easy. That video is brutal."

As we got to our cars, I looked over at Gorley and as he climbed into his Rolls Royce I said, "Believe it or not, I think I do believe him also."

As I said this, I wondered to myself, "If it wasn't Hugo and it wasn't the husband, who could it be? There weren't a lot of other potential suspects. If it wasn't one of those two, anyone on the ship could have had some role in her disappearance, which was a very unsettling thought since between the passengers and the crew, there were over 3000 people on board the Mardi Gras the night of Linda Weigand's disappearance. And now, of course, those people had spread all over not just this country but the whole world.

33

It was Friday, two weeks later, when the headless and limbless torso of a woman washed ashore on the beach at Cozumel, Mexico, near one of the three ports where the cruise ships dock. Portions of what appeared to be a black trash bag clung to the body. The remaining part of the body was badly decomposed and showed evidence of a shark having eaten parts of the body. One of the beachgoers who had found the body called the Mexican Federales. Two Federales officers pulled up to the body on the beach in a Jeep about an hour later. One of the officers came out of the Jeep, opened a black body bag and placed the torso in the bag. He then muttered some expletive in Spanish, and casually threw the body bag in the back of his Jeep.

I read the report of the discovery of the torso in the Miami Tribune-Gazette in a story written by Ken Hendricks on the front page of a special edition of the paper. The article stated that the state of decomposition of the body indicated that it had been in the water for at least several weeks. The Medical Examiner in Cozumel was quoted as saying that the cause of death was a bullet wound to the chest that had pierced the heart. Ken's article suggested that the body may be that of Linda Weigand, but until the DNA tests were completed, the article went on to say, it was not possible to say with certainty that it was her.

When I called Ken about the article, he said that from what he had heard from his sources, it appeared likely that based on where the Mardi Gras had been located and the tidal patterns on the night of Linda Weigand's disappearance, the body had come from the Mardi Gras.

"No one wants to speculate in print," Ken said. "But all the evidence points in that direction."

34

Mary Beverley was Linda Weigand's mother. Linda was her only child and she had raised her as a single mother while working two jobs as a waitress in a Denny's and as a shoe saleswoman at Macy's. She flew into Miami from Cincinnati to try to identify whether the remnants of the body that had washed ashore at Cozumel were those of her daughter. The police and FBI had also asked her to give a DNA sample to allow the medical examiner to compare her DNA with that from the body. The body had been transferred to Miami by courier aboard a private plane and it was now resting in the Miami-Dade County morgue.

Mrs. Beverley was a large woman, with a shock of yellow hair that looked like it had been colored with an entire bottle of French's yellow mustard. When she arrived in Miami she was wearing a flowered house dress that was cut low at the top, revealing her ample bosom. She spoke in a loud voice that seemed to carry for miles whenever she spoke, which was often.

On the flight from Cincinnati, she had caused a bit of a ruckus when she asked her seat mate on the plane, a potato chip salesman for Frito-Lay, "Have you heard about that missing woman from the cruise ship?"

After Mrs. Beverley explained what had happened, she asked him, "Honey, what are you doing tonight? After I'm done with the morgue, I'll have some time. How about we get together?"

The salesman jumped about two feet in the air, stood up and spent the rest of the flight in the restroom at the front of the plane. When the plane landed, he somehow managed to sit on one of the flight attendant's jump seats and exited the plane before anyone one else.

When Mrs. Beverley got off the plane at the Miami International Airport, she was greeted at the airport by a virtual phalanx of Miami-Dade police officers and a half dozen reporters, including reporters from the local ABC and CBS television stations. As she walked to the waiting police car outside the terminal, she held an impromptu news conference.

"Who do you think is responsible for your daughter's disappearance?" a young, handsome anchorman type from the local CBS station shouted at her.

"Well, honey, I have no doubt it was that sleaseball, Joe Hugo," she yelled back.

"She was a nice girl from Cincinnati until she met Hugo. She told me about all those outrageous sex games and drugs he got her involved with. To say nothing about all the booze. By the way, honey, what are you doing later tonight?"

The reporter actually blushed and put his head down. He was hoping this little exchange wasn't going out on a live feed.

"Now, don't be shy, honey. I'm just a regular gal from Cincinnati, Ohio."

Her comments about Hugo were exactly the type that the reporters had been hoping for. They always help boost the ratings when they are hyped all day long as so-called, "Breaking News." And because it was a ratings sweep month, she couldn't have come at a better time for the stations.

I watched the evening newscast that day where the Linda Weigand disappearance was the lead story and this exchange between Mrs. Beverley and the reporters was repeated over and over again, ad nauseum. Didn't the reporters have anything better to do than report on this obviously crazy lady? She wanted, no demanded, Andy Warhol's famous "fifteen minutes of fame." She was not to be denied that opportunity.

The DNA test results would take several weeks to be complete and even then some of the results might not be available for even longer. If the body was not that of Linda Weigand, it would make all the difference in the world for Joe Hugo. Now, if it was her body, well, let's just say, Hugo will have a helluva time beating this murder rap. Meanwhile, Hugo's plea at his final arraignment was due in just five days. I wondered why Gorley had taken no action to delay the arraignment at least until after the DNA results were in.

35

After my meeting with Hugo I decided that it was time to talk to Sergeant Boudreaux about the evidence she had gathered while on the ship and which undoubtedly formed the basis of the prosecutor's case against Hugo. I especially wanted to look at all of the videos from the night of Mrs. Weigand's disappearance. Somewhat reluctantly, I dialed her number and immediately heard her answer, "Boudreaux."

"Sergeant, this is Mario Morales," I said. "I wonder if I could drop by your office to talk to you if you have some time today about this Weigand matter."

"It is actually now 'Lieutenant Boudreaux,'" she said. "Sure, any time tomorrow will be fine."

"How about 11 tomorrow morning?"

"Fine, I will see you then."

Boudreaux was now located in the administrative offices of the Mariner cruise line just outside Miami. I had learned that she had recently been appointed the head of security operations for the entire cruise line. Obviously, she had done well for herself since I had been fired. Her office on the top floor of the building was small, but well-furnished with a large wooden mahogany desk, two leather-covered chairs and a nice view of the Miami skyline.

As I entered her office, I said, "Congratulations on the promotion, Lieutenant. I'm sure it is very well deserved. Very nice office, by the way." I said as graciously as I could.

"Why, thank you, Lieutenant. That's very nice of you. So, what can I do for you?"

"As you probably know, I have been retained by Mr. Bud Gorley, Joe Hugo's lawyer, to assist in his defense and help with the investigation into the facts."

"No, I did not know that," Boudreaux said rather unconvincingly.

"Well, the fact is that I have been retained by him. And what I would like to do is to see all of the tapes from the closed circuit security cameras aboard the ship the night of Mrs. Weigand's disappearance. I was hoping that you might still have copies of them. "

Boudreaux said nothing for a minute or so as she looked out the window of her office. "You know, I could tell you 'no', but you would be able to get the tapes from the prosecutor's office through the criminal discovery process before Hugo's trial. So, I'll let you see them here in our offices but I won't provide you with copies without a court order."

I reluctantly agreed to this condition although I would have preferred to have my own copies to study at my leisure.

"Okay, when can I see them?"

"How about right now?" she said.

I spent the rest of that day and part of the next day in a small, airless room, next to the mailroom, reviewing the tapes from the 250 cameras which were aboard the Mardi Gras. I looked primarily at the tapes from 12 a.m. until 4 a.m. on the night of Mrs. Weigand's disappearance. I looked closely at the tape showing Hugo and Linda walking the corridor and entering Hugo's suite. I noticed something strange about the tape. Hugo seemed to staggering as he walked down the hall and into his room. At a couple of points, it even appeared that Mrs. Weigand had to hold him up to keep him from falling over. I began to wonder how much he had to drink that night. I still hadn't talked to the bartender in the casino, so I made a note to contact him and hear what he has to say.

I also kept coming back to the tape of someone dumping a black bag into the water. Something on that tape struck me. While the tape showed the man carrying the bag down the corridor where the Hugo suite was located, it did not actually show the man coming out of the Hugo suite. I must have run the tape back a hundred times, but it was impossible to determine whether the man came from the Hugo suite. Also, there was no tape actually showing Hugo returning to his stateroom that night other than with Linda at 1 a.m.

"Very interesting," I thought.

In addition to those two tapes, I also reviewed several other tapes from that day. One of them, made in the afternoon on the day of her disappearance, appeared to show Linda Weigand on the Lido deck talking to a woman all dressed in black. Although the picture was very blurry, I was sure that the woman was Sun Li.

I had my suspicions since my conversation with her in the dining room the morning after Mrs. Weigand's disappearance that Sun Li knew a lot more about the disappearance. That tape seemed to confirm it---or at least it showed that she may have known Linda Weigand.

As I was leaving the conference room, I stopped by Boudreaux's office to thank her. I popped my head in the door and said "Thanks, Virginia, I appreciate your help."

She looked up from her desk and said, "Mario, you're quite welcome. And, just so you are aware of this. I had nothing to do with you being let go by Mariner. I had no reason to do that. I thought we were beginning to work well together after a bit of a rocky start."

"Well, that's very nice of you to tell me that. I felt the same way."

"One thing you should know: I did do a little checking and apparently the reason that you were fired was because someone, I'm not sure who, contacted the president of Mariner and specifically asked that you be terminated. Just thought I would tell you."

Very interesting, I thought to myself. Someone obviously wanted me out of the picture. But who? And why?

36

I went to Gorley's office the next morning. I thought he would be extremely interested in hearing about what I had observed on the tapes the day before. After waiting about an hour in the lobby, his assistant, Avery, finally ushered me into his office. He was sitting at his desk, looking at some documents. He looked up when I came in, but did not say anything, which I thought was rather strange.

"Bud, I am beginning to see a pattern here that you will find interesting," I said as I sat down on his guest chair.

I told him about my review of the tapes and the inconclusiveness of the key tape showing someone throwing a black bag overboard and the problems that Hugo was experiencing walking that night. I also explained what I had suspected about a possible Chinese connection to Mrs. Weigand through Sun Li.

After I had finished with my summary of what I had learned, Gorley said, "That's wonderful," as he twirled around in his large black leather executive chair and peered out over the Miami skyline. "Just wonderful," he repeated. "I'll be sure to tell Joe about these developments." With that, he turned back towards me, got up from his chair and ushered me out of his office without saying another word.

I was bewildered. I had assumed that Gorley would be ecstatic at the news about the tapes. Maybe the information would not lead anywhere, but at least it raised the possibility that it would create a reasonable doubt in the minds of the jurors at Hugo's trial.

37

As soon as Morales was out of his office, Gorley was on the phone calling Yao Lin. He had spoken to Yao only once since he had received the million dollar retainer. In that earlier call, on the day after the Mardi Gras had docked in Miami, Yao had told him that he was to make sure that he was present when Joe Hugo was brought into the police station following his arrest. Yao had also told Gorley that it was imperative that Hugo retain Gorley to represent Hugo. Gorley didn't ask how Yao knew that Hugo would be arrested. There had been a lot of speculation in the news media and among the lawyers at the criminal bar in Miami as to suspects in the disappearance of Mrs. Weigand, but no announcement had been made by anyone as to who would be arrested.

Gorley knew that making sure that Hugo retained him might be difficult and wondered what would happen to him if Hugo did not retain him. He assumed that it would not be good. So Gorley took no chances and he made sure he was there in the station house as Hugo was brought in, just as Yao had predicted he would be. And fortunately, Hugo did retain him.

Now, Gorley needed some more guidance from Yao. Morales seemed to be poking in all the right places. He also was concerned about being an accessory to murder now that it appeared that Linda Weigand's body had surfaced.

"Yao," Gorley began rather hurriedly, "It is

extremely important that I talk to you immediately. I have several troubling things to discuss with you. I have spoken to Lieutenant Morales and he has told me some things which concern me. Also, those body parts that were found off the beach in Cozumel, that was not part of the deal."

"Mr. Gorley," Yao interrupted Gorley, "I think you and I must meet in person rather than discuss these delicate matters on the telephone. Shall we meet at the Golden Lotus restaurant on SW14th Street in about an hour? I understand they have excellent egg rolls there."

"Fine," said Gorley, "I will see you then."

38

After I left Gorley's office, I decided that now was definitely the time to talk to the bartender from the casino on the night of Mrs. Weigand's disappearance to see what he recalled about Hugo's appearance that night. I thought he might have some information on the state of mind and physical condition of both Hugo and Linda. I knew that his name was Anton Cojoc. I had a copy of the ship's directory of permanent crew addresses and found out that he lived in a building in Little Havana near Calle Ocho, not too far from my own apartment.

It was an old building that had seen better days. Cojoc lived on the third floor according to the mailbox outside the building's front door. Because there was no elevator, I trudged up the three flights of stairs. I knocked on the door of his apartment, number 302.The door opened after just a few seconds and I was greeted by a beautiful young woman in a diaphanous, pink nightgown. It left little to the imagination, but the young lady did not seem to mind. I recognized her immediately as one of the dancers from the nightly musical show on board the Mardi Gras.

"I'm here to see Anton Cojoc," I managed to blurt out.

"Anton, some guy here to see you," she yelled as she disappeared into the other room in the apartment, leaving me alone in the doorway of the apartment.

A minute or so later, a man came out of that

room in black, boxer undershorts and a white beater tee shirt. Obviously, I had interrupted something here.

"Mr. Cojoc, I don't know if you remember me, but I'm Mario Morales, the former head of security on the Mardi Gras."

"Of course," he said as he opened the refrigerator and pulled out a can of Coors Light.

"Beer?" he said to me as he sat down at the small table next to the kitchen.

"No, thanks," I said. I could not really believe how nonchalant he seemed to be under the circumstances.

"Well, what can I do for you, Lieutenant? I assume you are not here just to pass the time of day," he laughed.

I explained to him that I was now working for Bud Gorley in connection with his representation of Joe Hugo and wanted to talk to him about the night of the disappearance of Mrs. Weigand.

"I understand you were the bartender on duty that night in the casino and that Mr. Hugo and Mrs. Weigand were sitting together at the bar at closing."

"It is true that I was on duty that night," he said, as his eyes wandered toward what I assumed was the bedroom. "Daphne," he yelled to the woman in there. "Don't get dressed yet, we will be done here soon."

I knew I only had a limited amount of time since he obviously had more important things on his mind so I plunged right into it. "Did you notice anything strange that night about either Mr. Hugo or

Mrs. Weigand."

"Well, there were lots of people who were drinking that night at the bar, so I am not sure."

"Do you remember anything?"

"I do remember a man and what looked like a much younger woman were sitting at the bar and laughing together. I don't know if that's who you are talking about. The woman was very pretty and the man was quite big and not very good looking. I am always surprised what some women will do for money," Cojoc laughed as he said this.

I then described Hugo and Mrs. Weigand to him.

"Yes, yes, I do remember now," he said, still eyeing the bedroom.

"Did you see anything strange that night between the two of them?"

Cojoc thought for a moment and then said, "Yes, I remember that after a couple of drinks, Old Fashioneds, I think, I saw the woman put something in the man's glass when he was not looking. I thought it was to help him later, you know, in bed. The man finished the drink and as he got up from the bar stool, he stumbled and almost fell over. I offered to help the young lady to get him back to his cabin. But she insisted that she could handle him. She then helped him out of the casino bar. She did leave me a very nice tip when they left. And that's it."

"Are you certain you saw the woman put something in the man's drink and not the man putting something in the woman's drink?"

"No," he said as he took a final swig from

the Coors Light and threw the empty can into a blue trash, recyclable bin in the corner of the room. Cojoc then stood up from the table, but continued, "She put something into his drink. I am certain. She was not even drinking any alcoholic beverage. She drank only ginger ale that night. I am sure. And if you will please excuse me, I have an important engagement I must attend to."

With that, he grabbed my arm and led me to the door of the apartment and ushered me into the hall. I could hear the deadbolt in the apartment click behind me as I walked down the hall, down the stairs and out into the street.

39

When Gorley arrived at the Golden Lotus Restaurant, Yao was already seated at a table in the corner of the room, underneath an ancient, ceremonial sword. Gorley immediately thought of the Sword of Damocles, but realized that it was probably hanging over his head and not Yao's. With Yao was the young lady Gorley had met in his office, Sun Li. The two large men packing guns who had also come with Yao to the initial meeting with Gorley were nowhere to be seen. But Gorley suspected that they were not too far away.

"Sit down, Mr. Gorley," Yao said. "As I told you on the phone, the egg rolls are superb here. I have taken the liberty of ordering a half dozen, two for each of us," he laughed. "You will enjoy, I am sure."

After biting into one of the egg rolls covered with Chinese mustard, Gorley started coughing rather loudly.

"Ah ha, Mr. Gorley, too spicy for you?"

"Yes, too spicy," Gorley managed to say before gulping down a glass of water.

Finally, Gorley was able to speak again and said, "Mr. Yao, I have to talk to you about what is going on with Mariner. Is it okay to speak in front of the young lady?"

"But of course," Yao said as he nodded in Sun Li's direction. "Of course."

"Look, I never anticipated that someone would actually be murdered. If I had known that, I never would have become involved in this whole plan."

"Oh, Mr. Gorley, you never asked. In any event, I am not sure what you are referring to."

"Why, the body parts that were found off the coast of Cozumel, of course. What else?"

"Mr. Gorley, we had nothing to do with that body. It just appears to be a fortuitous event from our perspective," Yao said as he finished a second egg roll. "I can assure you, Mr. Gorley, we had no one murdered," Yao continued. "Really, Mr. Gorley, you must finish your egg roll. Perhaps a little less mustard this time."

Gorley could not believe what he had just heard. "Are you sure, this was not all part of the plan?"

"Mr. Gorley, we do not believe in using force unless we absolutely have to.

"We Chinese prefer the path of least resistance. That is why tai chi is so popular in our country. If you ever come to visit our beautiful country, you will see young and old practicing the tai chi forms in the parks. It is really quite beautiful to see. You should try tai chi some time, Mr. Gorley. It will calm you down. Is there anything else?"

Gorley looked down at his plate and said, "Yes, there is one more thing."

"Yes," said Yao.

"Mr. Yao," Gorley went on, "this Morales guy you told me to hire to keep an eye on is turning out to be a real pain in the neck. He seems to know a lot about really happened that night or at least he is very good at speculating as to what might have happened."

"Do not worry, Mr. Gorley," Yao said, "we will address the Morales issue at the appropriate time. In the meanwhile, eat, eat. Have another egg roll. This time not too much mustard," Yao laughed as he crunched down on another egg roll slathered in the hot mustard.

40

The next day, Hugo was to have his formal arraignment before Judge Harold McFarland, a District Judge for the Southern District of Florida. Because the disappearance and now presumed murder of Linda Weigand had taken place at sea, the federal courts had jurisdiction over the case under federal maritime law. Judge McFarland was known as a stickler for details and for having a very short fuse. He loved to embarrass lawyers, particularly young and inexperienced ones. The rumor was that several lawyers, women----and men---- had been seen on various occasions running from his courtroom, crying. Even some experienced trial lawyers were said to have been shaken up by his treatment of them in the courtroom. I wondered how Gorley would fare in front of Judge McFarland, although I found it difficult to believe Gorley would ever cry over anything.

The lawyers who appeared in front of Judge McFarland privately referred to him as "Hardass McFarland" because of his treatment of them and their clients. One day while he was at the Union Club where he belonged and generally lunched by himself, Judge McFarland had overheard one of the lawyers passing by his table refer to him as "Hardass." Afterwards, he took great pride in the title and even had the name "Hardass" wood-burned on a plaque which he put behind his desk where only he could see it. It was a constant reminder to him of what he thought was his "duty": to knock some sense into the ill-prepared lawyers who appeared in front of him, none of whom ever seemed to pass muster.

What particularly irked him were those lawyers who refused to settle a civil case or, in a criminal case, take a plea bargain for their clients. He thought most trials were a complete waste of time, costing taxpayers money and keeping him from the golf course, where he was almost a scratch golfer. Besides which, if the parties did go to trial and the loser appealed to the Court of Appeals, his handling (or more accurately, his mishandling) of the case could result in a new trial. Judge McFarland hated nothing more than being reversed in his decisions by the Court of Appeals. When that happened, he always took it to be a personal affront. And it happened more often than not due to his heavy handedness at trial and in dealing with lawyers. More than once, the Court of Appeals had slapped his wrist because of the obvious bias in his rulings.

41

The purpose of a final arraignment is to have the defendant formally advised of the charges against him, and to plead "guilty" or "not guilty" to those charges. Usually, this is just a mere formality, frequently over and done within a matter of minutes. On this occasion Judge McFarland wasted no time as he entered the courtroom from the door to his chambers to the side of the bench and plopped himself down in his chair on the bench at exactly 9 o'clock. He was an imposing figure, with his grey hair combed in a large pompadour and with his bushy black eyebrows that covered his glowering black eyes. He looked like a silent movie leading man. Behind him on the marble wall was a huge seal proclaiming this to be the United States District Court for the Southern District of Florida. Judge McFarland banged his gavel and began, "Mr. Janosz," McFarland addressed the prosecuting attorney, "Are you prepared to proceed?"

"Yes, your Honor."

Tomas Janosz was the assistant U.S. attorney who had been assigned by the U.S. Attorney to handle the Hugo case. Janosz had emigrated from Poland with his family when he was twelve years of age. He still spoke with a slight Polish accent. Like many assistant U.S. Attorneys, he had ambitions to be a judge someday. The successful handling of a big case like this would surely give him some of the publicity he would need to get his name on the short list for the next vacancy on the district court. There was even a rumor that Judge McFarland soon might be soon stepping down from the bench so that he could devote himself full time to his golf game.

"Mr. Gorley, I assume that you and the defendant are also prepared to hear the charges against Mr. Hugo and enter a plea on his behalf," Judge McFarland said as he looked at the defense counsel table, peering over his half lens reading glasses.

Gorley stood up very slowly, rising from his chair at the defense table like a cobra unwinding from a basket at the bazaar at New Delhi. It was easy to see that his every move in the courtroom was carefully choreographed for the maximum effect upon the judge, the jury (when there is one) and the spectators as well. Next to Gorley sat Hugo who was wearing one of those hideous orange prison jumpsuits that made it hard to miss who was the defendant in the courtroom. Both his hands and legs shackled, Hugo had his head in his hands as Gorley stood up to address the Court. I almost felt sorry for the guy.

"Your Honor, I wonder if we might approach the bench. Something has come up that I think might be best discussed at sidebar rather than in open court."

"That's a rather strange request at this stage of the proceedings, Mr. Gorley. Do we really need to do that? "

"Yes, your Honor, I think it will actually move the proceedings along even a bit faster than normal."

"If you say so," the judge said dismissively. "Mr. Janosz, do you have any objection to a sidebar at this time?" McFarland was clearly pissed at this change in his protocol. I wondered if this was a wise move on the part of Gorley and more importantly for now, just what the hell was going on here. Gorley had not told me anything about the need for a sidebar or a change in plans from what I had assumed would be a perfunctory "not guilty" plea at this time.

Janosz turned and looked for guidance at his boss, the U.S. Attorney, Jeffrey Smith, who was sitting directly behind him. Janosz knew that would be his call and not his own. After a few seconds, Smith nodded his head and Janosz turned to the Judge and indicated his agreement to the sidebar.

"All right, gentlemen, approach the bench but let's try to keep this as short as possible. As you probably saw on my list of cases taped to the door to the courtroom, I have an extensive docket this morning and I haven't allotted much time to this case because it is only an arraignment."

The lawyers then all descended upon the judge's bench. I was in the third row of the packed courtroom, and I could not make out what was being said. I did note that all the parties, including the judge, seemed to be rather agitated. Several times, I did hear the judge say, "No,No.No," but I had no idea what had preceded the judge's negative comments.

Finally, after about fifteen minutes, the group at the bench broke up and each of the counsel returned to his respective seat at counsel table.

McFarland, looking quite pleased for a change, cleared his throat and said only four words:

"This case is continued." With that, he got up from the bench and disappeared out the side door into his chambers.

Outside the courtroom, there was a frenzy of activity. News reporters were lined up with their cameras and strobe lights on, ready to roll.

"What's going on here?" was the call that was repeated over and over again by the reporters as we left the courtroom and the courthouse. Those reporters were eager for some explanation for the continuance for their reports on the noon newscasts. Gorley smiled his most charming smile at the reporters but did not say a word. Neither did Janosz. The reporters were clearly disappointed.

"Where's the story now?" I overheard one of the reporters say to another.

"What's that Gorley guy up to?" came from another reporter as they rushed back to their respective satellite trucks to give their on the scene reports. I trailed Gorley into the waiting black limousine. As the driver pulled away from the curb with the smell of burning rubber and a loud screech, I asked, "What the hell is going on here?"

Gorley ignored my question and began texting on his IPhone. Gorley was as silent as he had been with the news media as we drove back to his office. Not a further word was exchanged between us.

42

Because Gorley for some reason had clammed up with me about what was happening, I decided to call on Lieutenant Boudreaux in her office to see if she knew what was going on. I had a feeling that her friends at the FBI had kept her well-informed as to what was occurring with the Hugo case. And I turned out to be right. She did know a lot more than me.

"Come in," she said graciously as she pointed to the chair in front of her desk.

"This is a little awkward for me," I began, "but I would like to know what is going on with Joe Hugo."

"Oh, I'm surprised you had not heard. Mr. Gorley has told the prosecutors and the judge that he expects that Joe Hugo will plead guilty to voluntary manslaughter."

I was stunned. I was completely blindsided by this change. All I could manage to say was "Why?"

"It seems that Hugo has said that he remembers very little about the night of Linda Weigand's disappearance," Boudreaux continued, "but he does remember Linda Weigand was in his suite about two o'clock in the morning and that they had a fight. He was very upset with her for marrying Weigand. All he remembers, he says, is that he pushed her and then he blacked out. When he woke up the next morning on his couch, he said she was gone and there was a small table turned over in the area where they had been fighting. And that was it."

"Did he see her body? And what about the black bag and throwing her body overboard?"

"He claims not to remember any of that. He claims he can't remember anything after pushing her. And by the way, the remains found off the coast of Cozumel were not Linda Weigand's. That has been confirmed by the DNA tests on her mother. What a crazy lady she is. One of those crazy publicity hounds who demand their fifteen minutes of fame. Apparently she was very disappointed that it was not her daughter and that the press no longer had any interest in her."

"So, there is no body of Linda Weigand?"

"That's right, but basically it looks like the prosecution is going to get a confession and that will be enough. That's why the prosecutor is willing to lower the charge from first degree murder to voluntary manslaughter."

"If the body did not belong to Linda Weigand, then whose body is it?"

Boudreaux answered, "The FBI is still looking into that. They are trying to find a match in their database. So far, though, no luck."

I just could not comprehend why Hugo was now admitting to the killing of Linda Weigand. There still did not appear to be sufficient evidence to convict him beyond a reasonable doubt even of voluntary manslaughter. I knew something else was at work here and I was determined to find out exactly what it was that led to this change of heart on the part of Hugo. I was also confused about why Gorley was so close-mouthed about this whole thing. It struck me as very odd for this lawyer, who prided himself on his ability to sway jurors in favor of his client, to just give up the ghost and have Hugo plead to this lesser charge of voluntary manslaughter. After all, I knew that even a conviction on that charge could carry a mandatory sentence of least at 3 to 5 years and maybe even considerably longer.

I decided I needed to talk to Joe Hugo myself to hear it straight from the horse's mouth.

43

I had a friend who worked as the head guard of the Miami-Dade county jail, Lee Tedesco. I had come to know him through one of those Cuban retirees I played chess with in Domino Park in Little Havana. Tedesco was his cousin and he had sometimes joined us. I decided to call him to see if he could get me in to visit Hugo alone, without Gorley.

I called the jail and after a short wait, Tedesco came on the phone.

"Lee, this is Mario Morales. I don't know if you remember me, but I used to play chess in Domino Park with your cousin, Victor Menendez."

"Oh, sure, Mario, of course, I remember you. I heard you lost your job on the cruise ship. I feel bad for you. What can I do you for? If you're looking for a job at the jail as a guard, I'm sorry to say that we're not hiring now. The county people have put a freeze on hiring. Damn budget cuts."

"No, Lee, I'm not looking for a job, but thanks for thinking of me. Well, I have sort of an odd request for you. You see, I'm working with Bud Gorley on this Joe Hugo case."

"Oh yeah, somebody said you was in here a few days ago with Gorley to see Hugo."

"Yeah, Lee, and that's why I'm calling. You see, I need to talk to him again. This time by myself, without Gorley. I have some information that I need to pass on to him and to get some information from him. I wouldn't ask if it wasn't real important."

"You know, Mario," Tedesco said, "I'm really not allowed to do this, but as a favor for you, I'll let you have five minutes with Hugo. I know you are working for Gorley, so I think it is all right."

"Thanks, Lee."

"I was a little surprised that Hugo decided to cop a plea in this case," said Tedesco. "You know, I'm a pretty good judge of character and I just didn't see this one coming at all. He struck me as the kind of guy who would fight tooth and nail, balls out, to keep out of prison. And with Gorley as his attorney, it's even more confusing to me."

"You are not the only one who was surprised," I responded as I started to hang up the phone. "There are a helluva lot of surprises in this case."

Little did I know then just how true that would be.

44

I arrived at the jail the next morning at 7 a.m. and asked to see Hugo. Tedesco had made arrangements with the guards on duty since he was not yet there. I was told by one of the guards that I would have to wait for a few minutes.

I sat in the waiting room for almost an hour glancing at ancient copies of Sports Illustrated Magazine. As I was flipping through the well-worn pages of one of the magazines, I looked up and saw Robert Weigand leaving the jail. Now why would Weigand be here at the jail? I wondered. The only explanation that made any sense to me was that he was here to see Hugo. But why? I have got to ask Hugo about that.

Finally, I was taken by a guard back to the attorney's room where I had met with Gorley and Hugo a few days before. When Hugo entered the room, he looked like he had not shaved in a week and seemed to me to have lost a few more pounds, maybe even 10 or 15.

I decided not to fool around with Hugo and before Hugo even sat down at the table opposite me, I asked sharply, "Why did you decide to plead guilty?"

Hugo looked away for a moment and then turned and stared back at me. I could clearly see that he was stunned by my question.

"I must have done it, that's why," came his reply.

I pondered that response before saying,

"What do you mean you must have done it. Did you do it? You don't remember doing it?"

"To be honest with you, I don't remember anything from that night. I had had too much to drink, I guess and so I must have blacked out. "

"Did you ever have that happen before?"

"You mean where I blacked out after drinking too much?"

"Yes, of course that's what I mean."

"Yeah, well, you know I played college football."

"Yes, I know you played for the University of Miami."

"Well, I had quite a few concussions there and sometimes, even now, I feel the effects of those concussions. It's not like it is today. The helmets are much better and the doctors know a lot more about concussions. Back then, they would hold up a couple of fingers and if you recognized the number correctly, the coaches would send you back into the game."

"What happens if you drink too much? Do you black out right away?"

"A couple of things usually happen. Sometimes, I get these uncontrollable rages. I just can't control myself. I throw things around and just feel like I'm going to explode."

"How often does that happen?"

"Not often, but sometimes when I have too much to drink, it kinda sets me off. You know what I mean?"

I began to wonder; maybe he did kill Linda Weigand. Obviously, given this information, it was entirely possible, he blew up, had a fight of some sort with Linda Weigand and, in a rage, killed her either intentionally or, more likely, by accident.

"What do you remember about that night?"

"The last thing I remember was playing blackjack at the same table as Linda. I was losing quite a bit of money, maybe five or six thousand dollars. We then decided to have a few drinks at the bar. I ordered a couple of Old Fashioneds and I'm not sure what Linda had."

"What happened next?"

"I'm not really sure."

"Do you remember going back to your suite?"

"Not specifically," he said. "But I must have."

"Do you remember having Linda Weigand in your suite?"

"I guess so."

"You guess so? So, you do not specifically remember her being there at all?"

"Look, I'll be honest with you. I've always had the hots for Linda. She and I got it on a few times after making those crazy television ads together. Who wouldn't after you saw her hanging out all over those cars? You know, one time we made out in the backseat of an Odyssey van. I later sold it as a 'demo'. You bet I was more than a little pissed that she decided to marry Weigand."

"Were you pissed enough to kill her?"

"Not intentionally. No. But as I said, sometimes, this thing just comes over me and I can't control it."

"So, you think that's what happened that night?"

"I guess so."

I had interviewed a lot of suspects when I was with the LAPD and knew that during their interrogation, it was surprisingly easy sometimes to manipulate them into making admissions. And not all of them were true. I found that it was not just the kid from the streets who would make the admissions. The more rational the person, the more intelligent the person, it seemed like the easier it was to make them admit what seemed to be the only obvious conclusion based upon the irrefutable facts that you presented them with, even if those facts were purely hypothetical or even completely untrue.

"Who came up with the scenario that you had a fight with her that night and you accidently pushed her over and she struck her head? Was that you or the police?"

Hugo thought for a moment, "I guess it was one of the cops. He told me all the evidence pointed to that as being the only way it could have happened. Yeah, it was one of the cops. Duffy was his name, I think. Yeah, Duffy."

I knew Duffy, of course, from our days on the LAPD and particularly from the time I sat on the review board for interrogation of that Hispanic boy who confessed to a crime he never committed. It had been rumored that that Duffy always got a confession. No, not just some times, but always.

"You know, Duffy knew all about my first wife." Hugo continued.

"What about your first wife?"

"Well, shortly before we got divorced, she got a PFA against me."

I knew, of course, that a PFA was a protection from abuse order that the courts would enter to keep someone (usually a man) away from another person (usually a woman) because of the potential for violence against that person.

"How did that come about?" I asked.

"That's what's sorta ironic. I was messing around with one of the receptionists at the dealership. Nothing really major, but my wife found out about it. She confronted me about it one night when I got home from the dealership after midnight reeking of Chanel No.5. My wife only wore Poison so she knew I was with another woman. Damn stupid of me. I went into a rage during our argument and slapped her across the face. That's all I did, I swear. I had too much to drink and immediately regretted it. She was a good wife too. But she called the cops and they issued me a citation. Next thing I knew, she called her lawyer and got a PFA against me and that was it. I had to move out of the house right away. We got divorced about six months later and I had to pay through the nose."

"Did Duffy know all of that?"

"Yeah. Yeah, he knew it all. I had tried to get the whole thing expunged from the public record years ago. But my lawyer got the expungement all botched up and information about the PFA even found its way into the local newspapers. I think somebody was out to get me. Had to be something like that."

"So, as I understand it, you don't remember any of those kinds of things actually happening with Linda Weigand, but you are willing to plead guilty to voluntary manslaughter, am I correct? Does that make sense to you?"

"Look, I had no choice," Hugo said as he buried his head in his hands. "I had no choice," he repeated. "No choice. They were going to charge me with first degree murder unless I cooperated and took a plea to voluntary manslaughter. And they also had that crazy money laundering thing to hang over my head. They said I could maybe get an enhanced sentence if I was convicted at trial. I wasn't exactly sure how that went, but I knew it would be bad."

"Did you tell Mr. Gorley about the circumstances of your confession?"

"Yeah."

"What did he tell you?"

"He told me to plead and he would get me the best deal that he could."

"Did he tell you what that best deal was?"

"No, but I trust him. I have to trust someone. He's a lot smarter than that shyster I had in the case with my first wife. He's supposed to be the best damn trial lawyer in the country. Besides which, I'm paying him an arm and a leg. I'm sure he would give me the best advice. I'm not happy about the prospect of going to jail, but if I did it, I guess it's only right. And maybe, Gorley said, just maybe, he might even be able to get me house arrest or probation or something like that. He says he knows the judge real well and he thinks he can get him to be a little lenient to me. Hell, that's why I'm paying the great Gorley those big bucks."

I wondered whether Gorley was just blowing smoke with that statement concerning Judge "Hardass" McFarland, but decided not to say anything to Hugo about him. Given his reputation, it seemed unlikely he would have mercy on a killer and would likely sentence Hugo to the maximum sentence and not the minimum. In Florida, if I remembered correctly from a couple recent high profile cases, the maximum penalty for voluntary manslaughter was fifteen years. That's a long time by anyone's measure.

"One thing I don't understand," I said, "is why you didn't tell me any of this when we first met?"

"Oh yeah, Gorley told me specifically not to tell you about what happened with this Duffy guy."

"Did he tell you why he didn't want you to tell me?"

"He just said that the fewer people who knew about it, the better."

The guard came in and announced that our time was up. I got up and started towards the door. As I did so, I said, "One more thing. What was Robert Weigand doing here?"

"What do you mean?"

"When I was in the waiting room waiting to see you, Mr. Weigand was leaving the jail. I had assumed he was here to see you."

"If he was, I never saw him. Nobody told me he was here. You're the only person I've seen this morning. Gorley is supposed to come by later today."

"When he gets here, I would appreciate it if you didn't mention that I was here to see you this morning."

"Why's that?"

"I just don't want him to get his nose out of joint that I came here to see you without him. You know how these damn lawyers are. They're so compulsive and wanna do all this legwork themselves. I would rather just fill him myself on our conversation after he meets with you."

"Yeah, sure, I'll keep quiet."

"Thanks. I'm glad we had this conversation."

"You think I'm doing the right thing, don't you? About pleading guilty," Hugo yelled over his shoulder as the guard led him out of the room.

I did not respond.

"Hey man, I'm sorry about the way I treated you back on the ship when you came to see me. You see, I was under a lot of pressure," Hugo said. "But that's no real excuse."

As I was leaving the jail, I checked the sign in book at the entrance. I was looking for Robert Weigand's name. I found his name and opposite his name was the name of the prisoner he had been visiting: Victor Ortiz. Ortiz was my predecessor on the Mardi Gras. Now, why in the world was Weigand visiting Ortiz?

45

I knew, of course, that Sergeant Duffy was a detective with the homicide division of the Miami-Dade police department. I also knew him from his days with the LAPD. Apparently, the FBI had let him do the questioning of Hugo, which I thought was a little unusual. The FBI usually likes to keep everything in their own court and not share it with the state authorities. But then again, the FBI probably wanted a confession in order to tie this case up in a neat, little bundle and do so quickly. And Duffy was definitely the man to do that. I was sure that the FBI was getting a lot of pressure from the cruise line industry. After all, a murder on a cruise ship was definitely not good for business. The cruise business had already been tarnished by all the fires and other incidents which had recently occurred aboard cruise ships from all of the cruise lines, big and small. It was tough enough getting people to cruise without them also having to worry about getting murdered aboard ship.

I knew of Duffy's reputation as a tough, no holds-barred interrogator and knew it would do little good to try to talk to him about Hugo's supposed "confession." Duffy had been well-schooled in the so-called Reid Technique of interrogation.

The Reid technique was developed by a former Chicago cop named John Reid. The technique involves several steps, all of which are designed to insure that the interrogator will get a confession from the suspect. First, the interrogator observes the demeanor of the suspect. If he appears anxious or makes certain body movements during questioning, the interrogator assumes that the suspect is guilty and he must get a confession since it is always the best evidence to convict. The interrogator then begins with innocuous questions that are designed to get the suspect off guard. After a series of those, the interrogator may lie to the suspect by claiming to have more evidence on him than really exists or by downplaying the moral effects of what the suspect is accused of doing. The interrogator also has to keep rejecting all denials made by the suspect and repeatedly insist to the suspect that the suspect is guilty and should confess because "it will make you feel better" or it is "good for the soul."

Sometimes, if there is more than one suspect, the interrogator also may lie and say that the other suspect has already implicated the interviewee. As Duffy's track record showed, this type of questioning technique worked exceedingly well. I myself refused to use the Reid technique because I thought it was duplicitous and was more likely to result in false confessions than in genuine confessions. But a lot of cops disagreed.

The more I thought about it, the more it sounded like Hugo's confession was in reality all Duffy's idea and that Duffy had used the Reid technique to a "T" with Hugo. Surely, I thought Gorley would have figured that for himself. I was astonished that Gorley had not filed a suppression motion before Judge McFarland to keep the confession out of evidence. To me that was the obvious thing to do. Yet I guess I shouldn't have been too surprised

since nothing in this case seemed to follow the obvious path.

46

My doubts that Hugo had killed anyone, much less Linda Weigand, continued to grow. It all seemed too pat. Hugo had a history of violence against women and Duffy undoubtedly used that history to convince Hugo that he murdered Linda and threw her body overboard. And then there was that video that seemed to show Hugo doing just that. But there were just too many unresolved threads. I decided that I needed to talk to Weigand again. For one thing, I was very curious as to why Weigand was at the jail to see Victor Ortiz the morning of my meeting with Hugo. What was that all about, I wondered? What connection did they have? All these thoughts were tumbling through my head as I tried to figure out exactly what was going on here.

Before I could talk to Weigand, first, of course, I had to find Weigand. Surprisingly, I was able to find a phone number and an address for him in the Miami Beach phone directory. I thought most people had dropped their land lines altogether. I called the number listed but only got one of those messages saying that the number was no longer in service. No surprise there. The address was in Miami Beach and I drove over there.

When I got to his apartment building, I was told by his landlord that he had not returned to his apartment since the Mardi Gras had docked and that most of his clothes were gone. For some reason, I had a hunch he still might be staying in a hotel in Miami. I called several hotels in the Miami area, asking if Robert Weigand was staying there. On the 12th call, I finally struck pay dirt. My hunch had paid off. The receptionist who I spoke to would not acknowledge specifically that Weigand was staying in the hotel because, she said, it was against hotel policy to identify any guests for privacy reasons. But then she offered to connect me to his room. Go figure. I decided to visit the hotel in person rather than call him.

The Remington Hotel was a small boutique hotel in South Beach. It was painted a vibrant pink and yellow on the exterior walls and those colors also dominated the colors on the walls and upholstered furniture in the small lobby. I had never been to the hotel before but I had heard that the lobby bar was a very active gay bar most nights, but particularly on the weekends. There was a large sign written in lavender letters on the wall behind the bar that read "Anything Goes." I could only imagine what that could mean.

"I'm here to see Mr. Weigand," I said to the desk clerk, a very thin young man with a pencil thin mustache and slicked back blonde hair, obviously dyed a yellow that was never seen in nature.

"Let me check," he said as he turned back to the computer sitting on a small table behind him.

When he returned from checking the computer, he said, "I'm afraid you just missed him. I came on duty only a few minutes ago, but the records show that he and his wife checked out about fifteen minutes ago."

"He and his wife?" I said.

"Yes, they were here several weeks."

"Are you sure about that?"

"Yes, I saw them almost every day."

I wondered if this guy ever read the newspapers.

"Are you aware that Mrs. Weigand was reported missing several weeks ago while on a Caribbean cruise?"

"No, never heard that. Weird," the clerk said. "That's weird."

"Well, thanks anyways," I said as I started to leave but then said, "You wouldn't happen to know where they were going, would you?"

"I don't, but I think our bellman might know. I am sure he would have helped them with their bags." The desk clerk then called over to the bellman who was standing at the far corner of the lobby, having a cigarette behind a tall ficus tree.

"Philip, this man would like to know where the Weigands were going when they checked out of the hotel. Can you please help him?"

Philip, a tall African-American with a long, black goatee and cornrows, shook his head.

"Sure, I helped them get a cab and they told the taxi driver to take them to the Miami airport. They said they were going to the international terminal. That's all I know," he said.

"By the way, what did Mrs. Weigand look like?" I asked.

"She was really something," Philip said. "Tall, black haired. We don't usually get those kinda white chicks in this hotel. No sir, she was built like a brick shithouse. Oh, I'm sorry, excuse my French."

"Now, Philip, you bad boy," the desk clerk chimed in. "Naughty, naughty," he said as he rubbed his index fingers together in the universal mark of shame---for five year olds and younger.

I thanked Philip and stuffed a 10 dollar bill into his hand.

"Man, you isn't gotta do that. But thanks, I can always use a few bucks around this place."

I handed him another ten for his trouble. If his information turned out to be true, it would be worth a whole lot more, especially for Joe Hugo.

47

I had seen the picture of Linda Weigand that Captain Vivaldi had shown me the day of her disappearance. I distinctly remembered that she was tall, but that she had bright red hair, not the dark hair the hotel bellman had described. And in any event, Linda Weigand was dead. Or was she? There was no body. Could she still be alive and wearing a black wig? Or did Mr. Robert Weigand decide to move on with his life with another woman? I tended to doubt that, but you never know, you just never know.

I drove as fast as I could to Miami International Airport in my rented Ford Fusion. As usual, traffic was backed up everywhere. It took me almost an hour to get there. After parking my car in the short stay lot, I ran into the lobby of the international terminal. My only hope in catching up with them was to get to them before they went through the security line.

As it was a busy Friday afternoon, the security line snaked around the terminal and out the door. I quickly scanned the line, hoping I would see them. At the beginning of the line, I saw Weigand and a tall brunette going through the x-ray machine. I thought about calling after them, but decided it would be fruitless at that distance. I did watch them as they headed towards the international departure gates.

I returned to the main lobby and checked the departures screen. The only international flight leaving within the next few hours was a direct flight to Shanghai.

I immediately called Bud Gorley. He was not in, I was told by his assistant. I left him a message telling him about who I had seen at the airport. He did not return my call that day or the next.

48

In light of all I had learned from Hugo concerning his confession, my suspicions about Bud Gorley began to grow exponentially. What exactly was he up to? I knew of his reputation as a suave bulldog in the courtroom, willing to do almost anything to get his client off. Yet, he was willing to allow Hugo to take the rap for a crime I believed Hugo did not commit, if there even was a crime at all. And now Weigand is taking off to China with a tall brunette. Something was fishy here, very fishy. But how could I get to the bottom of all this?

Then, I had an idea.

Diego Van Gogh was a good friend of mine. He had that rather unusual name because his father was a Dutch immigrant and his mother was Mexican-American. They had met in New Mexico, married and had two children, including Diego. I had met Diego at a law enforcement conference years ago in San Francisco. Like Diego, I also had a mixed heritage. My father was Mexican-American, while my mother was Irish. Diego and I hit it off immediately and we had stayed in touch over the years. I was glad we had now that I needed his help.

Diego was now the sheriff of a small town outside Miami, where he had moved some ten years ago. He presided over a force of ten deputies. Mostly, he and his deputies spent their time tracking down speeders on the Interstates and chasing drug runners who tried to use his small town as a trading post on the way up North. I thought I could trust

Van Gogh and decided I would enlist his help in trying to find out what was going on with Hugo, Gorley and the Weigands.

"Come right in, Lieutenant Morales. It is so good to see you again." Van Gogh gestured toward me as he closed the door to his office behind me. Van Gogh's office was filled with numerous antiques which he had collected over the years. He was fascinated with old swords and at least a dozen hung on the walls of his office. There were Russian sabers and Civil War swords, both Union and Confederate. The office was dominated by a large mahogany desk that sat on a platform about 6 inches off the ground. That platform enabled Van Gogh to look down upon anyone who was sitting in front of his desk. Although only about 5 foot six inches tall, the platform gave Van Gogh a commanding presence, which he savored. Those who sat in front of him felt like they were sitting in a hole.

"Diego, thanks for agreeing to meet with me, I know how busy you are."

"I am never too busy to meet with a friend. Would you like a Montecristo?" he said, offering me a large, fat cigar. "These are the same ones that Winston Churchill favored, the real thing too, straight from Havana, courtesy of the drug lords we all hate." He laughed as he lit the cigar and handed the match to me and I did likewise.

"What can I do for you, my friend? I was very sorry to hear about you losing your job on the Mardi Gras. That seemed like a good fit for you at this stage of your life. But I also heard you were working for that 'defender of freedom,' Bud Gorley. What a shyster," Van Gogh said as he blew a smoke ring up to the ceiling which was already quite black from many such puffs. "Sorry about talking about your boss like that, but I just don't like the man. He has been responsible for allowing more drug runners to go free than any man in Florida. But, I have to give him credit. He is very good in the courtroom. Very good."

"I need your help on a matter. It involves Joe Hugo and Bud Gorley," I said, interrupting his little tirade against Gorley.

"I heard about your involvement in the Hugo case. I was a little surprised that you would join up with Gorley, but I guess any port in a storm."

I just nodded my head as Van Gogh continued,

"Isn't Hugo going to plead guilty to killing his mistress, that Weigand woman?"

"Yeah, he is. But I happen to think he is innocent."

"Innocent, that's a strong word, Mario. Innocent, which one of us is truly innocent," Van Gogh mused as he sat back in his large, black executive chair and took another long puff on the Montecristo.

"Look, Diego, I'm not even sure there has been a murder, "I said.

Van Gogh looked rather stunned when I said this. "What do you mean, no murder? The Weigand woman is dead, isn't she?"

"I'm not convinced she is dead," I said. I first told him the story of the circumstances surrounding the confession obtained from Hugo by

Duffy.

"So, you think Hugo was railroaded into confessing to something he never did? I, of course, know all about Duffy and how it is said he can get even a saint to confess to killing his mother. He is one bad dude," Van Gogh acknowledged. "But, on the other hand, he does help to serve justice----- sometimes."

"If a murder even happened in this case," I said.

"Why do you think this Weigand woman is not dead?" Van Gogh asked.

"I believe that I just saw her with her husband at the airport, taking off for some foreign country, I assume. Probably China, from what I can figure out. She was wearing a brunette wig, but I believe it was her."

"Who is behind this grand conspiracy that you think is out there?" Van Gogh said in a tone that suggested that he was not buying my theory as to what really happened.

"That is where I need your help. I don't have a badge anymore and I can't really find out much more information without one."

"If I were to help you, I, of course, would be putting myself on the line. And if there is such a grand conspiracy as you are suggesting, I could be squelched like a bug myself. After all, like you, I am just a poor little half-Mexican. In order to achieve all of what you are suggesting, there would have to be some very powerful people behind it. We would both be playing with fire." Van Gogh shook his head as he said this and my stomach sank as I realized that he probably was not going to give me the help that I needed.

I tried reassuring him. "I really do need your help and if anyone's head is on the chopping block, it will be mine."

"Let me think about it." Van Gogh said after about a minute as he continued to puff on the Montecristo. "It is a very interesting situation. But I must think about it before I plunge right into it. After all, I have my own responsibilities here in this county. I must 'serve and protect' the people," Van Gogh laughed. "Yes, that is what I do, 'serve and protect.'"

"I appreciate you taking the time to meet with me, Diego," I said. "I hope you can help me, but I will understand whatever you decide to do."

"Be very careful," said Van Gogh as we shook hands at the door. "It's a minefield out there."

Truer words were never spoken. I left Van Gogh's office and began walking towards my rental car, which was parked on the street across from the sheriff's office. As I began crossing the street, I automatically hit the remote door button on the keychain to open the door. When I did so, I heard a click but it did not sound like the usual click that you hear when the door is unlocked. No, this had a very different sound---a very ominous sound. Next thing I knew I was on my back on the ground as the rental car exploded into what seemed like an a million pieces of flying metal and glass. The shock wave from the blast blew out almost every window on the block.

I lay on the ground about 25 feet away from the car which had ignited in flames shooting some 20 feet or so in the air. People sometimes say that these incidents occur in slow motion. Not this one. I never knew what hit me. One second I was standing and walking to my car, the next, I was flat on the ground, having no idea how I got there.

Van Gogh came running out of his office, came over to me and said, "Are you all right?" Several other deputies also ran from the office. One of them was carrying a fire extinguisher and began spraying the burning Ford with foam, although it seemed to do little good as the flames continued to shoot up towards the sky.

"As all right as I can be when someone has just tried to kill me," I said as I stood up very wobbly and dusted myself off. I shook shards of glass and metal from my hair and felt something wet, blood I assumed, on my hands as I wiped my forehead. In the distance I could hear sirens blaring and I soon saw a fire truck pull up next to the still-burning car. Three firemen jumped out of the truck and began hooking their hoses up to the hydrant on the corner. In what seemed like less than a minute, they had the fire out. The once new blue Ford Fusion that I had rented was now just a mass of twisted, burned metal. The thought crossed my mind: how am I going to explain this at the Hertz counter where I had rented the car. Fortuitously, I had actually taken the non-insurance insurance they offered. I never do that, just as I never buy the extended warranty on anything I purchase. I guess this time I just had a feeling.

Before I could say anything, Van Gogh said to me, "I will join you in your crusade to find out what is going on here. We will get to the bottom of this. Nobody can try to kill my friend and think they can get away with it. Come, my friend, I will take you to the hospital. You have a very bad cut on your forehead. Very bad." I said I would be all right, but Diego insisted.

Diego drove me to the nearest hospital, where they checked me out in the Emergency Room. The ER doctor said the wound to my head was superficial, despite all the blood, but they wanted to hold me at the hospital overnight for observation to determine if I had a concussion. I was glad to be in the safety of the hospital that night and slept like a baby.

49

The next day, after I had returned home from the hospital, I got a call from Gorley who asked if I could meet with him in his downtown office. Gorley did not tell me why he wanted to see me, but only that I should be in his office first thing the next morning. I thought maybe he had another assignment for me on the Hugo case. I was definitely wrong there.

"I heard someone tried to kill you a couple of days ago," Gorley said as I entered his office at about 8 o'clock the next morning. "I was very sorry to hear about that. Very sorry."

"Yes," I answered.

"Any idea who would want you dead?"

"No, not as far as I know."

"Do you think it was retribution from one of the people you had arrested when you were on the LAPD?"

"Could be," I said. "Could be."

"Well, in any event, I hope they catch whoever was responsible. I'm sure you don't feel very safe now. I surely don't want to put you in more jeopardy at this point. Given that, I thought it best that we part ways. You know, I was going to have to let you go anyways. The Hugo case, as you know, is basically over with. You know, of course, Hugo is going to plead guilty to voluntary manslaughter and I've worked out a pretty good deal for him with the prosecutor, some jail time, sure, but mostly probation. I think I can even get Hardass

McFarland to go along with it. You know it really might have been an accident."

Obviously Gorley wants me out of the way, I thought.

"Look, I feel bad for you. Here is another ten thousand dollars for your help and trouble," Gorley said as he handed me another white envelope stuffed with hundred dollar bills. Once again those Benjamins.

"That's a lot of money," I said. "I'm not sure I've done enough to merit that much."

"Of course you have. And if this bombing has anything to do with this Hugo matter, which I sincerely doubt, that's even more reason you should have the money."

I thought that was a curious choice of words, but said nothing about it. "Well, I guess that's it," I said as I put the fat envelope filled with money into my inside coat pocket.

"Look If I need some help in the future, I'll be sure to call on you," Gorley said as he ushered me out the door to his office and into the hallway.

"I think I know what's going on," I said under my breath to no one in particular but, just loudly enough to make sure Gorley heard me, as I closed the door to Gorley's office.

I lingered in the hall outside Gorley's office for a few seconds, long enough to hear Gorley get on the phone. I heard him dial very quickly.

"I think he knows what's going on," I heard Gorley say. "You had better take care of business soon. We can't have this little twerp mucking up this deal at this late stage of the game. There is just too much at stake here."

50

This was now the second time I had been fired from the Hugo investigation. And the first time someone had tried to kill me. Although Gorley had fired me, I knew I had to continue to find out what really happened to Linda Weigand and more importantly, why. Thoughts of my sister, missing all these years, continued to haunt me.

I decided to contact Ken Hendricks to see if he had learned anything more that might be of help in unlocking this puzzle.

"Ken, this is Mario," I said.

"Hi Mario," Ken said. "Are you all right? That's crazy about that bombing of your car."

"Yeah, pretty good. I have a pretty hard head," I laughed.

"I'm glad you called, I have a little piece of news that you might find interesting."

"Yeah, what's that?"

"I checked some court records and found out that Bud Gorley is representing Victor Ortiz in connection with a drug bust."

"You're kidding," I said. Ortiz, of course, had been the chief of security on the Mardi Gras whom I replaced when he was fired after two of his security guards were found smuggling drugs aboard the Mardi Gras, apparently for a Mexican cartel.

"If I were you, you might want to talk to him," Kendricks said.

"Of course. I'll try as soon as possible."

51

The next day, I returned to the Miami- Dade County jail again and asked to see Ortiz. I told the guard at the gate that I was working for his lawyer, Bud Gorley, and needed to clarify something with him. My little ploy worked.

I met with Ortiz in the same small lawyer's conference room where I had previously met with Joe Hugo on two occasions. Ortiz was brought into the room by a burly black guard. Ortiz was a small man, shorter than me, only about five feet four inches tall, with curly black hair and a large mustache, black as coal. Ortiz sat down across the table from me but did not offer his hand to shake. I could see the skepticism in his eyes.

"My name is Mario Morales," I introduced myself. "Like you, I was once the chief of security aboard the Mardi Gras. Now, I'm working with your lawyer, Bud Gorley and he asked me to stop in and ask you a few questions." Another lie, but I figured that this was the only way I could get him to talk.

"So why do you want see me? Gorley didn't tell me anything about you coming. Usually, he comes himself. Is he too busy to see me now that he is representing that Hugo character?"

I thought it best to ignore the question and just ask him what I wanted to know.

"I want to get some insight into why the Mardi Gras was being used for running drugs from Mexico, specifically cocaine."

"Who said it was being used that way?" Ortiz said, as he waved his hands in the air.

"Was it?" I said as I stared straight into those black eyes.

After a few seconds, Ortiz finally responded, "Look, I was just a very small cog in the big machine." Again, he waved his hands around in the air.

"What do you mean by that?"

"You don't really think I ran that operation by myself, do you? If so, you are more stupid than I thought when I first saw you."

I ignored the insult and continued on.

"Well, who did run it, if you didn't?"

"You would never believe it if I told you."

"Why don't you try me? It could really help your case."

I pulled out a small notebook from my pocket and began taking notes as Ortiz talked. This time, in case something unforeseen happened to me, I wanted to have a file to document what I had learned.

The story Ortiz told me, I have to admit, caught me completely by surprise. Later when I got back to my apartment, I typed up my notes on my computer:

Ortiz says that about a year ago he had been approached by a Shanghai businessman, Yao Lin, who had a very different interest in the Mariner Cruise line. Yao told Ortiz that he had been involved in trafficking in opium in the golden triangle of Asia for many years. He was very successful in that enterprise. Now, he wanted to extend his circle of influence to include the United States of America.

Yao knew that illegal drugs frequently are brought into this country through Florida. The smugglers frequently will come ashore in small boats with kilos of cocaine and other illegal drugs from Columbia. Many boats and people (to say nothing of the cocaine itself) are lost in the process, whether at sea or when they come ashore. The U.S. Coast Guard patrolled the waters off the coast of Florida, constantly looking for those smugglers. Ortiz said that Yao had taken a cruise on the Mardi Gras a couple of years before. He saw that there were many lapses of security aboard the ship and that he saw the Mardi Gras as the perfect vehicle to expand his drug business to North America, with very little chance of being caught.

Yao saw an opportunity of a lifetime to acquire a trade route just like Marco Polo had done to China some five centuries ago. It took Yao several years to amass the capital to make an offer to buy the Mariner cruise line. He had watched the fortunes of the Mariner and was very pleased to see that they were on the verge of bankruptcy. Yao felt that would ensure that he could get the cruise line for the cheapest price.

One of the first people he contacted concerning the purchase was Ortiz, who was then the head of security on the Mardi Gras. It was important to him to get Ortiz to cooperate with his plan. Ortiz was more than happy to go along with Yao, particularly because he was himself in a dire financial position. He was a very heavy gambler who frequented the blackjack tables in the casinos on the Indian reservations in Florida. Several times *he had lost more than $2000 in a single night.*

Ortiz had recruited several of the security guards to assist in the smuggling operation. They were the actual "donkeys" who would carry that coke from the sandy beaches of Cozumel to the shores of the United States. The two security guards whom had been caught red-handed were his main couriers. When they were arrested, Ortiz and Yao were both deprived of much of their incomes.

Ortiz also referred to a new drug, something called "spice" that Yao was very interested in bringing into the United States. Ortiz said it was a very powerful form of synthetic marijuana that is often used by high school students. This was the new Far Eastern "spice trade." I remembered that Ken Hendricks had also mentioned spice. Ortiz also said that because so much cocaine was being brought into the United States through Puerto Rico, Yao wanted to maintain another way station in Cozumel to keep the drug enforcement people guessing.

Unfortunately for Yao, Ortiz was fired because of the arrest of the two guards on board the Mardi Gras. Because of Ortiz' expertise in the drug smuggling operation, Yao decided he would still retain Ortiz and to continue to pursue the Mariner Cruise line. When I was hired to replace Ortiz, it was important to get me out of the way. Joe Hugo created another stumbling block when he decided to put in an offer for the cruise line. Yao had to find a way around both of us in order to implement his plan.

Ortiz claimed that was all he knew. He asked rather plaintively whether that would help his case.

I told him, "Sure, I'll be sure to tell Mr. Gorley all you told me and I know he will be able to use it to your advantage in court." Of course, I had no intention of telling Gorley anything about this conversation.

As I left the conference room, I could see Ortiz smiling. He really did think these admissions would help his case. I almost felt sorry for the guy.

Before I closed the door, I had a hunch and asked him, "The other day, did a guy name Robert Weigand visit you in your cell?" Of course, the day I had visited Hugo, I had seen Weigand leaving the jail. I originally thought Weigand had visited with Hugo, but when I had checked the records, I knew that he was actually there to visit Ortiz.

"Yeah, I didn't know the guy, but he said he wanted to talk to me."

"Did he say why?"

"Yeah, he claimed he worked for that Chinese guy, Yao, and he wanted to make sure that everything was okay."

"What did you understand he meant by that?"

Ortiz thought for a moment and then said, "He said Yao wanted to make sure that I didn't tell anyone about his involvement in the drug smuggling operation."

"What did you say?"

"I told him no, of course not."

Suddenly, Ortiz realized that he had just told me the whole story.

"You do work for Gorley, don't you? And the attorney-client privilege or whatever that is, covers everything I told you, right?"

I assured him on both counts. I was lying, of course, since I no longer worked for Gorley, but I wasn't about to tell him that.

52

My ploy had worked. Even though there were still some gaps in determining what was going on, I now knew for certain that Gorley had to be deeply involved in something larger than just the Hugo case. There must be a ton of money at stake here for Gorley to get involved. After all, he did have his reputation as the "go-to guy" for major civil and criminal cases not only in Miami, but all of South Florida. But then again I remembered what Ken Hendricks had told me about the extent of Gorley's money problems. Maybe he needed the money even more than I thought and that anyone else knew.

I called my friend, Sheriff Van Gogh, and told him about my conversations with both Gorley and Ortiz.

"Mario, you had better be awful careful out there," Diego said. "You are obviously dealing with very powerful forces that will stop at nothing to get what they want. They tried to kill you once. You may not be so lucky next time. You don't want to be inside your car the next time it explodes," Van Gogh said.

"Amen to that," I answered. "Amen."

Van Gogh continued, "I wanted to make sure that I told you something I think you will be happy about. I was able to convince my friend at the federal prosecutor's office to get me a copy of the keycard usage records on the Mardi Gras for the night of the disappearance of Mrs. Weigand. I have the disc containing those records that he gave to me.

You want to come and take a look at them? My buddy's ass that got these records for me is really on the line for this, so I owe him big-time. I did give him a box of Havana cigars for the time being. He seemed pleased."

I knew that each time anyone uses a keycard to open a door on the ship, it is electronically recorded on a computer which can later be accessed to determine when a door to a cabin or other area was opened or closed. I had asked Diego to see if he could get me a copy of those electronic records. I thought that those records might be helpful in determining what exactly happened the night that Mrs. Linda Weigand disappeared aboard the Mardi Gras.

"I'll be right over," I said.

I jumped in a cab and was in Van Gogh's office in about 15 minutes.

"Have you looked at the records?" I asked as soon as I got to Van Gogh's office.

"I've glanced at them but I'm not exactly sure what to look for. I assumed you would know."

"Hugo was in stateroom no. 71," I said, "so let's start there."

It took a while, but I scrolled through the file of documents on the computer and eventually found the door record for Stateroom 71 for the day and night of Mrs. Weigand's disappearance.

I looked down the long list of entries. There were several dozen the day of Mrs. Weigand's disappearance.

"Look at this," I said, as I showed Diego the entries for Hugo's stateroom.

"These records clearly show that Hugo never left his stateroom after 1 a.m. and no one entered his room until 8 o'clock the next morning when the steward came to clean up. The steward's keycard leaves a different record than the passenger's."

Van Gogh scratched his head and said "And the meaning of all this?"

"So, if Mrs. Weigand was killed and thrown overboard, and I don't think she was, there is simply no way that Hugo could have done it unless he is the invisible man. The videos show the two of them heading towards Hugo's cabin at 12:58 a.m. His last use of the keycard was at 1:00 a.m. when presumably he and Mrs. Weigand entered his cabin. Because the door to his cabin was not opened after that until the morning, he could not have left his stateroom and no one entered his room through the door. So that could not be him in the video carrying the black bag. My guess is that the records will show that it was the cabin next door that had been opened at the time of the video showing the man with the black bag." The cabin next door belonged to the Weigands.

I quickly checked the records and the search confirmed that it was the Weigands' cabin that was opened at the exact time of the video showing the man with the black bag.

"That man in the video must be Robert Weigand," I said.

"Somebody is obviously framing Hugo," said Van Gogh. "But who would want to do that and why? And what has happened to Mrs. Weigand?"

"I think I know who and why they were

framing Hugo. It just became very clear to me. Who stands to benefit the most if Hugo is out of the picture and in jail? The only thing I am not sure of is how Mrs. Weigand was able to get out of the Hugo cabin without registering on the door's records."

"Who do you suspect is responsible for all of this?" asked Diego.

"You may not know this, but Hugo had a bid in to purchase the entire Mariner cruise line in the bankruptcy proceedings. It looked like a done deal until he was charged in this case with the murder of Linda Weigand. All of a sudden, he's out of the picture. And who steps in: a large Chinese conglomerate, Shanghai Blue."

"So you think the Chinese are behind this?"

I first told him about my conversation with Ortiz and then added: "I'm almost positive they are. When I was on board the ship the morning after the disappearance of Mrs. Weigand, there was this beautiful Chinese woman who sat down with me at breakfast. I had actually had a few drinks with her the night before at the Captain's party. I'm wondering now if she was trying to size me up. She claimed to be named Sun Li, but I could find no evidence that anyone with that name was on the ship. She seemed to know all about the disappearance and supposed murder of Mrs. Weigand even though we had tried to keep it under wraps. I'm pretty sure that I saw her again the day we docked in Miami and she was with a group of Chinese who looked like businessmen."

"From what I've heard, I do know that these Chinese play hardball, but do you really think they would kill a woman, and frame another person for the murder just to buy a ship or two?," asked Diego.

"You forgot to add and try to kill me," I said. "But, first of all, I don't think Mrs. Weigand was murdered. I believe the woman I saw yesterday at the airport going down the international terminal was Linda Weigand, alive and well, and with her husband. If we are able to find a way to check their travel plans, I would bet that she and her husband are in some resort in China or maybe Hong Kong, laughing their asses off at the rest of us. The other factor that leads me to the conclusion that the Chinese are behind all of this is that the Chinese were the first to jump in and make an offer to buy the cruise line when Hugo was arrested and his bid was deep-sixed," I explained.

"For all this to fall into place for them, these Chinese would need to have a pretty good understanding of both the American criminal and civil justice system, wouldn't they?" Van Gogh asked.

"You're right, exactly. That's where I believe Bud Gorley fits into the picture. Nobody knows more about how to game the legal system than the great Bud Gorley. He hired me supposedly to assist him with the case but really I think he hired me in order to keep me close at hand so he could keep his eye on me for the Chinese."

"Mario, this all sounds great, although most of it, I think, is pure speculation on your part. Anyways, how are you going to prove any of this? Short of a confession from the Chinese or Bud Gorley, it seems like there is not much you can do. This door thing is obviously helpful to Hugo but the guy has already confessed and is going to take a plea bargain to a charge of voluntary manslaughter in just a few days. And once that happens, there's really not too much you can do to help him."

I knew that Van Gogh was right. "That's why we have to act quickly. If I can get Gorley talking, I might be able to get him to admit the whole thing. He has such a big ego, he will probably want to show off how intellectually superior he is to all the rest of the world and especially to me."

"So what if he does admit to you to some elaborate scheme as you surmise, it's just your word against his."

"Not if I'm wired up to record everything he tells me."

"That's pretty risky, don't you think? If he finds out that you are wired, you're a dead man."

"I think I have an idea how I can pull this off without getting killed."

"I just hope it works," said Van Gogh.

"So do I," I said to Van Gogh. "After all, my life depends on it."

53

I had promised to keep Ken Hendricks in the loop as to what was going on. I called him shortly after I left Van Gogh's office and told Hendricks of my plan.

He laughed when I told him. But it was a nervous laugh, like he knew it was risky, not of the "ha-ha" variety.

"Do you really think you can get Gorley to admit everything?" asked Hendricks.

"I don't really know myself, but I have got to try."

"What can I do for you?"

I explained my plan in detail to Ken and hoped that he would follow through with what I had asked him to do. If not, I would be in big trouble.

Ken then explained to me that he had been doing some digging on his own about Shanghai Blue and what he found was even more disturbing.

"You know this Shanghai Blue that's apparently behind all this, they own a chemical plant in Shanghai that is used to make this synthetic marijuana. It's ultimately owned through a series of dummy corporations by the Chinese government. They apparently distribute this stuff through a center right here in Florida. I was able to confirm that a lot of it was marketed towards kids as a cheaper and safe form of marijuana. But apparently it is just as addictive as even some stronger drugs, like cocaine."

"Holy shit," was all I could manage to say

when he finished.

"And that's not all. According to a report issued by the DEA, that I was able to find while doing my research, the proceeds of those sales are being sent to Yemen, Syria, Lebanon and Jordan. The Feds are concerned that once the money is over there in the Middle East, it is going to terrorist organizations, including Al Qaeda."

I told him that Ortiz had mentioned the drug to me but that I had no idea what a significant problem it was. Upon hearing this, my sense of urgency increased at least tenfold. I had to act quickly or it might be too late to stop the Chinese.

54

The next day, at about 2 o'clock p.m., I appeared unannounced at Bud Gorley's downtown office. To drive over there, I had rented another car from Hertz to replace the bombed out Ford Fusion. The clerk at the desk told me that the only car available was a three year old Ford Fiesta, about the size of a Volkswagen Beetle. When I went to the rental car lot to get my car, I saw row upon row of shiny new, full-size cars parked on the Hertz lot. I guess they were taking no chances with me this time.

I was carrying a small Sony digital recorder in the inside pocket of my sport coat, which I wore especially for this occasion. I had it set to record whenever anyone spoke. My plan was to record my conversation with Gorley and then turn the recorder over to the FBI. I doubted that Gorley would suspect I was recording our conversation but if he did, I had my Colt .22 "throwaway" strapped to my left leg in an ankle holster. I thought it unwise to wear the 99mm. That was probably a mistake in retrospect.

Gorley's office was in a tall, elegant, all glass building that reflected the hot Florida sun. As I was driving there, I wondered how drivers on the nearby freeway could see with the glare from the reflected sun in their eyes.

When I got to his office, Gorley's assistant, Avery, told me Gorley was too busy to see me that day and suggested that I come back another day. I asked if I nonetheless could wait for him. She said "sure" but then repeated that it was unlikely I would be able to see Gorley that day. I sat in the reception area for almost four hours reading the Miami Herald and working on the crossword puzzle. As usual, the newspaper was filled with stories of various murders and drug busts around the city. In the classified section of the paper, I happened across the legal notice for the upcoming sheriff's sale, which was due to be held in just two days. One of the items up for sale was the Mariner cruise line. Apparently, the bankruptcy court had made arrangements with the sheriff to handle the sale and it was clearly going forward.

At around 6 p.m., after everyone else had left for the day, Gorley emerged from his office and invited me into the office. It was now dark outside and most of the lights in the office had already been turned off.

"What can I do for you, Lieutenant?" Gorley said. "It is so good to see you again. I was afraid we left on bad terms the other day. Hopefully, I can make amends." He sounded very gracious, but I also sensed that he knew I was there for some purpose that was not going to make him very happy.

"Would you care for a cigar?" he continued. "I have some real Montecristoes, which I understand you like. You know, the best ones used to be made in Havana. But I find that the quality of those cigars is just no longer there. Quite frankly, I think the Dominicans make a much better cigar right now. Don't you agree?"

I nodded my head in feigned agreement but waved off the offer of a cigar, despite the strong urge I had for a nice cigar right now. Especially, a Montecristo.

"Would you care for a drink, then?" Gorley asked as he pushed a button on the shelf of his book case and a marble-topped bar suddenly appeared out of the book case. He poured himself about two inches of Jack Daniels and threw in a couple of ice cubes that clanged against the glass.

"You sure you won't have one with me," he said as he drained the glass of Jack Daniels in one swallow.

I decided not to waste time, "How did you get Hugo to confess to a murder that never happened?" I asked.

Gorley walked over behind his desk, sat down and swiveled his chair towards the Miami skyscrapers outside his windows and said quite earnestly, "I don't know what you are talking about. Joe Hugo killed Linda Weigand. He admitted that. Sure, he claims now that it was an accident or that he doesn't remember what happened. Who's gonna believe that story? Whatever his story, Linda Weigand is just as dead, isn't she?"

"Then why did I see her boarding a plane to China with her so-called, grieving husband just two days ago." Of course, I hadn't actually seen the Weigands board the plane to China, but I thought it would be a good bluff.

"You must be mistaken," Gorley said firmly as he turned around in his chair to face me.

"No, it is you who is mistaken if you thought you could get away with this. I know you are representing the Chinese company, Shanghai

Blue, in the bankruptcy proceedings where they are trying to buy the Mariner cruise line. Joe Hugo thought he had the deal all wrapped up, but the Chinese wanted the cruise line to use in their drug smuggling operations and would do anything to get him eliminated from the picture. You were using Hugo as a stooge, claiming he was a murderer in order to get him out of the way so the Chinese could step in and make the acquisition."

"Lieutenant, everyone is entitled to representation under our legal system, including the Chinese," laughed Gorley. "It seems like you know a lot more than you should. And that kind of knowledge can be deadly. Or maybe you are just bluffing. Either way, that can get you killed, Lieutenant. So be careful with your accusations."

I decided to ignore his little diatribe and I challenged him, "The other thing I can't figure out is how you got Hugo to be your client?"

Gorley laughed again. This time though he paused for what seemed like a minute but was probably only a few seconds before finally answering: "That was the easiest part of all. Hugo was out of his mind when he learned he was going to be arrested and charged with the murder of Mrs. Weigand. I just happened to be there as the police brought him into the station house following his arrest." Gorley laughed as he said this.

He then continued: "Of course, I knew all about what was going on with the Weigands. This Chinese fellow, Yao Lin, told me everything. He was the one who told me that I had to position myself in a way that Hugo would have to see me. I

218 · AJ BASINSKI

vaguely knew Higo from the Yacht club were we both belonged and I hoped that he would recognize me from the club or my television ads and appearances. And sure enough, he recognized me immediately. He asked the guards if he could talk to me in private and they let him come over to me. He then proceeded to beg me to represent him. I told him that I was very busy, but I would be willing to take him on because I believed in his innocence. That and a two million dollar fee—upfront. He was more than willing to pay that for my extraordinary talent as a lawyer." Gorley smiled as he said this.

"By the way," he added, "I know all about your little tete-a-tete with my client, Victor Ortiz. He called this morning and told me all about that little charade you pulled the other day, claiming that you were still working for me. Ortiz told me about it as soon as he had a chance to make a phone call. That was rather stupid on your part, don't you think." He laughed and continued, "You can be charged with the unauthorized practice of law."

"Do you plan on turning me in to the Florida Supreme Court disciplinary board?" I countered.

"Very funny, Lieutenant. Very funny. No, I have some other plans for you."

I continued to pursue him to get the full story, as it was clear that he was more than willing to talk about how clever he was. "How did you get involved with the Chinese?"

"Before I answer any more of your silly-ass little questions, open up your jacket."

Obviously, he was on to me. He must have

suspected that I might try something like trying to record him. I had definitely underestimated him. I knew I had to act quickly and reached for my gun in my ankle holster

Before I could get to it, Gorley pulled a .357 Magnum pistol from his desk drawer and pointed it directly at me and told me to put my hands up into the air. I did as I was told.

"Open the goddamn jacket," Gorley virtually screamed. I opened my jacket and Gorley reached over and found the recorder in the inside pocket. He then tossed the recorder into a large document shredder next to his desk. He turned the shredder on and the recorder was ground up to dust with a loud shudder.

"So, you thought you could trap me, little man. I could see where you were going with this little conversation from a mile away. Now we can talk. But keep those hands up. If you take them down, I will have to shoot you."

As I sat there, he kept the gun trained on me and I knew he meant it. But now he was even in a more talkative mood. "Those Chinese bastards came to me," Gorley said. "This Chinese dude named, Yao Lin, or at least that is what he said was his name, called me and asked to meet with me. He claimed he was an assistant Chinese trade representative to the United States. I agreed to meet with him and Yao told me about the plan to acquire the cruise line the very next day. They trusted no one. They even had me followed. Yao's company, Shanghai Blue, had been working on a plan for several years to enter the cruise line business in the

United States. They particularly liked the Mariner line because its ships cruised the Caribbean. I suspected from the very beginning that they were going to use the ships to smuggle drugs or at least something illegal. Yao later confirmed that they were introducing a new drug into the United States, something called 'spice.' By the time he told me that, I was too far into it to back out. Yao also told me that they had already retained the former head of security for the Mardi Gras, which they particularly favored. That was our friend, Victor Ortiz. I knew that Ortiz was a small time cocaine runner and they asked me to represent him. Ortiz had apparently promised them the world, but then ended up in jail."

I knew, of course, that Ortiz had been the prior head of security on the Mardi Gras. His firing and the actions of the two drug runners that had been caught all made sense to me now. Ortiz had been running cocaine for years and the Chinese wanted to use his expertise to broaden the operation to make it even more profitable and easier for them to smuggle drugs, which it would be if they had their own cruise line and dedicated security officer.

Gorley was not done and he continued, "The Chinese were all set to make an offer for the cruise line in the bankruptcy court when Hugo stepped in and made an offer to buy Mariner. The Chinese knew that so long as an American businessman was in the picture, their bid would probably be rejected in favor of Hugo's bid, particularly in light of the rising sentiment against Chinese investment in the United States. So, they needed to get Hugo out of the way and they hatched this little scheme to frame him for Linda's disappearance and presumed murder. When Yao revealed to me the details right before the news broke about Linda Weigand's disappearance, I thought the whole thing was rather crazy. But the more I thought about it, I figured, 'what the hell.' Nobody really gets hurt here."

"What about Joe Hugo? You don't think he's been hurt by all this? The guy could go to jail for 3 to 5 years, maybe even 15 if Judge McFarland takes a hard line with him even for a voluntary manslaughter plea. They don't call him 'Hardass' for nothing," I interjected.

"Oh, hell, a little jail time will probably do him some good. You know he had served time in federal prison years ago when he was convicted of money laundering. He'll do just fine in prison. You know most of those prisons are just like country clubs these days, filled with lawyers, accountants, stockbrokers and all kinds of professionals. You name it. Hell, even Martha Stewart did time and she came out bigger than ever with her products." Gorley laughed again. He was now clearly enjoying himself.

"What about the Weigands? How did the Chinese get them to go along with this little scheme? And what's in it for them?"

"That was a little tricky. But the Chinese dug up some dirt on both of them, some petty crimes when they both were kids. Surprisingly, both of them had checkered pasts. These Chinese are ruthless. They got them to play along and they offered each of them a million dollars and a safe haven in China. Who could resist that?"

"What about you? Why did you decide to become involved? In some ways, you had the most to lose if something went wrong with the plan."

Gorley briefly turned towards the ever-darkening sky outside his window, but still kept the .357 Magnum pointed at me. He turned back and said: "Money. The root of all evil," he laughed. "Look, despite appearances, my legal career probably is close to being over. I've been riding my reputation so long, my ass is sore. Too many new gunslingers coming along who are stealing the legal business that should belong to me. You have no idea how much pressure I'm under. My house, my car, my wife, my kids. It costs a bundle to live the lifestyle I have. Of course, you wouldn't know anything about things like that, would you?"

I just nodded my head in agreement with everything Gorley said.

"Do you have any idea how much those Chinese entrepreneurs were willing to pay me?" asked Gorley. "Millions, millions. And all of it, tax-free. These Chinese don't issue IRS Form 99s. They gave me a million dollar retainer. In cash. Do you believe it? And what they offered to pay me on top of that was much more than even I could make during the rest of my career practicing law. And a million times more than you could ever make playing security guard aboard a silly little cruise ship. Let's face it, you were like some mall cop, dealing with petty little crimes that nobody really cares about. A stolen towel, maybe, or at worst, a stolen wallet. Mostly though, you are just cleaning up after the passengers. You ought to be glad you are off that goddam ship."

I did not comment on this soliloquy. I thought it best to keep quiet and let him talk.

"So now you do know everything," Gorley said finally. "I told those Chinese bastards you were on to them, but no, they wouldn't listen. And then when they finally did believe me, they botched taking care of you when they had the chance. I never really thought they would try to kill you. I just thought they would scare you off the scent. Obviously now, I have no choice but to finish off what they had begun. And, Lieutenant, I assure you that I won't make the same mistake."

"What about those body parts that washed ashore at Cozumel? Who do they belong to?"

"The Chinese told me that they had nothing to do with the body in the black bag on the video from the ship or those body parts. I'm not sure that I even believe them on that. According to Yao, that was just another happy coincidence, giving even more credibility to the charges against Hugo. When I told the Chinese about the video, they were ecstatic. "

If the Chinese were not responsible for the body in the bag, then who was? And whose body was it? These were questions I asked myself and I hoped I would be around to learn the answers.

"Lieutenant, I decided that we are going to go on a little cruise ourselves. But only one of us is coming back. And by the time they find your body, if they ever do, I will be in Hong Kong, drinking green tea and getting a massage by one of those beautiful Chinese masseuses."

Gorley motioned to me to get up from my chair. He then pulled a large roll of duct tape from his desk. He was obviously well-prepared.

"Put your hands behind your back."

I did as I was told.

He then wrapped the tape around my hands and pulled it tightly around my wrists.

"Now, sit down again."

Gorley ripped off another strip of duct tape and placed it over my mouth. He *had* thought of everything.

He then took a pair of scissors and slit the pant leg of my trousers where I had my .22 taped to my leg.

"I thought you might try something like this, asshole," he said as he tore off the .22 and put it in his jacket pocket. "Get up," he ordered and then he led me to his private elevator, which he could access directly from his office. The elevator took us to the fifth floor in the parking lot where Gorley parked his cream-colored Rolls. The lot was deserted now except for his car.

Gorley opened the trunk of the Rolls and ordered me to climb in. After I did so, he slammed the trunk shut and I was in the dark of the trunk, trying to figure out my next move. Obviously, my options were limited. My best chance and maybe my only chance was to try to talk him out of whatever plan he had for my demise.

I could barely hear the Rolls engine start up but felt the car move forward. As it did so, I rolled around inside the trunk and hit my head on the spare tire. Blood started to drip down my face in a warm trickle. This was the second time in just a few days my head had been struck and bled. It was not a good omen.

55

Gorley drove for what seemed like an eternity before the giant Rolls glided to a stop. Gorley opened the trunk lid and pulled me out of the trunk. It was now completely dark but I recognized the area where we were as the Foster Yacht Club. It was located in probably the most remote part of the docks. Only one other boat was docked nearby. I assumed it was Hugo's yacht since Gorley had said they were neighbors at the yacht club.

Gorley led me down the pier. I could hear the water splashing against the pylons as we walked across the pier. Gorley still kept the .357 trained on me as we walked slowly down the pier. At the very end of the pier was a large tri deck boat, all oak and brass. It looked like it was at least a 45 footer and maybe more. It reminded me of something out of the Great Gatsby. I could just see Jay Gatsby piloting it through Long Island Sound. But this was no novel. And anyways, Gatsby ended up shot by an irate husband and drowned in his own swimming pool. That was not an image I much favored at this moment. Not at all.

As we prepared to board the boat, I glanced at the name of the boat written in what looked like one foot high, gold leaf letters on the stern, "Legal Beagle." Beneath the name was a painting of Snoopy wearing a Captain's hat with what looked like a British barrister's white wig beneath the hat. Very amusing, I thought. Very amusing.

"Get on board," Gorley ordered and the two

of us climbed a metal ladder to board the boat. The boat was quite luxurious, I thought. Gorley had spared no expense in furnishing the boat. The furniture on the boat was of the kind you might see in a mansion in West Palm Beach, something right out of Architectural Digest.

After we climbed to the top deck, Gorley told me to sit on the floor near the Captain's chair.

"Have you ever seen a more beautiful boat than this? Cost me over $5 million a few years ago. It is said to have once belonged to that Miami mob boss, Meyer Lansky. You know, from the Godfather. I had to completely redo it after I bought it. Cost another cool $2 million to get it shipshape. And you know how many times I've used it since? Twice, exactly. Twice in over two years. Do you believe it?" Gorley sounded incredulous as he spoke, not quite believing all the money he had spent on a beautiful boat he never actually got to use.

"We are going to take a little spin on my boat and as I told you before, only one of us will be returning. So, enjoy the ride while you can."

Gorley trained the gun on me and sat down in the tall captain's chair on the third level. He hit the ignition button. As he did so, the two large Mercury engines, each capable of 400 horsepower, fired up simultaneously, with a loud roar that reverberated up and down the docks.

He then steered us out of the harbor, moving the boat quite slowly at first. When we were about a quarter mile from the docks, Gorley reached down and tore the duct tape from my mouth.

I knew that this was my last chance. "Now, you don't have to do this," I said, as Gorley pulled back on the throttle and we soon seemed to be flying over the dark waters of the Atlantic Ocean. I continued, "You can probably find a way to beat this rap. A smart lawyer like you always knows some loophole. You could turn state's evidence against the Chinese. These Chinese are making money hand over fist with this new drug, spice, and the proceeds are being used to fund terrorist organizations in the Middle East. Hell, you could be a hero for turning them in."

"I don't really care at this point. You don't understand," said Gorley. "This little transaction was how I thought I could make enough money to get myself out of this money pit I put myself into. The only other way I can make money is by practicing law. Do you think they would ever let me practice law again here in Florida or anywhere else for that matter after my involvement in this matter?"

Gorley clearly was desperate but I wondered if he could really murder me. I thought I would test him.

"Look," I began, "do you really think that you can kill a person?"

"You know, I have always wondered about that. I've seen and actually represented so many murderers and I have always been fascinated by how their minds operate. Most of them have absolutely no remorse about their victims. That's why they can kill again and again."

"But you are not one of those people," I said. "Don't you understand, you are just being used by the Chinese? Do you really think they will take care of you if this whole thing blows up, as it will? Hell, they will just throw you away like the little paper inside a fortune cookie."

"Shut up," he yelled. "Just shut the fuck up."

I could tell that I was finally getting to him and maybe, just maybe, it would save my life.

As we plunged headlong into the night, about ten minutes out to sea, I could see the lights from what looked like a ship in the distance. Gorley also looked up and I'm sure that he also saw the lights of the ship that was bearing down on us.

Suddenly, the sky came alive with two sets of flashing lights. I could also hear a siren blaring. I knew then it was a Coast Guard cutter that was approaching us and what I assumed were two Coast Guard helicopters in the night sky.

"Shit," Gorley said, as he also apparently saw the Coast Guard cutter and helicopters. "Shit, shit, shit."

Gorley grabbed me by the neck and threw me down the ship's ladder to the deck below. He gunned the motors and headed out to sea as fast as his boat could take us.

I was slightly woozy from being flung down the ladder and it took a moment before I realized what was happening. Gorley was making a run for it.

"You'll never make it," I yelled to Gorley.

"Why don't you just shut the hell up," retorted Gorley. "This sucker can beat just about anything that floats and maybe even some things that can fly."

Gorley turned the boat to the starboard and we took off at what seemed to be at least 70 knots. As we began pulling away from the outgunned Coast Guard cutter, the twin Mercury motors started sputtering and after just a few more seconds, the boat itself came to a complete stop in the water. We were now drifting in the Atlantic Ocean about fifteen miles out to sea.

"Sonofabitch," Gorley yelled. "Sonofabitch. I told that dumb bastard harbormaster to always make sure my boat was fully-fueled because I might need it someday. Do you believe it, we ran out of gas!"

I could see the two Coast Guard helicopters approaching the boat even more quickly than before. As they got closer, one of the helicopters shined two spotlights on the boat, partially blinding me at first. Next, I heard a voice from one of the helicopters:

"This is the United States Coast Guard. Mr. Gorley, put your weapon down and put it down now. Get on the boat's deck and stretch out in the prone position on your stomach. Go, do it now."

I saw Gorley look up at the choppers and point his gun in their direction. It looked as though he was going to shoot it out with the Coast Guard using his .357 Magnum. But then just as suddenly, I saw him pull down the gun and point the gun at me.

"You know, I really should kill you, you little bastard. If you hadn't have been snooping around, this whole thing would have gone off as smoothly as a baby's rear end. And nobody would have been any worse off."

As he said this, Gorley then pulled the gun up and put the gun into his mouth and pulled the trigger. The force of the gunshot propelled him into the water backwards. I clambered to the top of the stairway and I watched as his body floated away trailing blood. Like the yacht itself, he was now dead in the water.

The Coast Guard cutter pulled up alongside the yacht and a Coast Guard warrant officer jumped aboard the yacht.

"Are you all right, Lieutenant Morales?"

"I guess so. I couldn't believe he did that."

"What do they say, 'Desperate men do desperate things,'" said the warrant officer, as he removed the duct tape from my hands.

"Thank God, you guys were out here."

"A friend of yours warned us to be on the lookout for the Gorley yacht and told us he thought you were being held hostage by Gorley"

"A friend of mine?"

"Yeah, some reporter, Ken Hendricks was his name. Do you know him?"

"Yeah, sure, I know him." So, Hendricks had really come through for me. I learned later that after I had told him of my plan to confront Gorley, he had followed me to Gorley's office. When he saw Gorley leave his building in the Rolls, he suspected I was with him, so he followed Gorley's car to the docks. When he saw Gorley pull me from the trunk of the Rolls and lead me down the pier to his yacht, he called the Coast Guard.

About a half hour after Gorley shot himself, two Coast Guard divers fished Gorley's body out of the water and pulled   him on board the cutter's deck, covering him with a white sheet. The cutter then towed the Gorley yacht to shore.

56

For the next two days, the FBI debriefed me on my discussions with Gorley. Fortunately, I was able to reconstruct the entire discussion I had with Gorley. Based upon the information I supplied them, the FBI executed search warrants on Gorley's home and office and obtained his phone records. When they went to arrest Yao Lin for his involvement in the scheme, he claimed diplomatic immunity and left the country, leaving behind Su Li. I found out that she also went by the name Suzy Nelson, which was why I couldn't find her name on the passenger list the day of Linda Weigand's disappearance.

The FBI was able to track down the Weigands in Shanghai where they were living in virtual poverty. The large Chinese conglomerate, Shanghai Blue, which was behind the whole scheme had reneged on the two million dollars they had been promised and the Weigands were trying to eke out a living. Robert had tried to get a job selling cars at the local Mercedes dealership, but the job had fallen through at the last minute when the owner of the dealership found out he had been selling Hondas in the U.S.

The United States Justice Department requested the extradition of the Weigands from China. The Chinese government readily complied and denounced the Shanghai Blue conglomerate for an excess of capitalism. After their return to Miami, both of the Weigands were charged with multiple counts of fraud for their roles in framing Hugo for the alleged murder of Linda.

Because Linda Weigand had not been murdered and was very much alive, Hugo's new lawyer petitioned the court for his release and the dismissal of all charges. The court granted the motion and Joe Hugo completed the purchase of the Mariner Cruise Line shortly after he was released from jail. He paid $180 million for the cruise line and he thought it was a great bargain. He promised he would bring back the line to its old luster.

I was rehired by Hugo to serve as chief of security aboard the Mardi Gras with a substantial boost in pay. Hugo had offered me the job as chief of security for the entire Mariner cruise line, but I refused to accept the job. Virginia Boudreaux was doing a good job, I told Hugo: "Let her keep the job." I preferred, I told him, to be a simple cop, a "mall cop", as Gorley had said, and did not want to become some administrative bureaucrat. Police work, I realized, was all I knew. And that was quite enough.

Ken Hendricks did not write a story about my problems with PTSD and my addiction to prescription drugs. I am forever grateful to him for that. Instead, he wrote a series of articles about the Chinese connection to drug trafficking and its connections to terrorist groups in the Middle East. He did not win the Pulitzer Prize for the articles, but he did leave the Miami Tribune Gazette shortly afterwards and is now working for The New York Times.

57

There was one piece of the puzzle that still needed to be filled in. And it just bothered the hell out of me: Whose body was it that was found floating, limbless and half decomposed, near Cozumel? The FBI had more or less lost interest when it was determined that it was not Linda Weigand's DNA. When I called Philip Benson, the Special Agent in charge of the Weigand investigation, he told me that he did not think there was any connection between the body and the Mardi Gras.

Quite frankly, I was astounded. It seemed an unlikely coincidence to me. But then again, Linda Weigand had been located alive and well. End of story as far as the FBI was concerned. That was the only reason why they had been brought in. Their job was done since the case was now in the hands of the U.S. Attorney for prosecution. I was told by one of the technicians that the FBI had run a DNA search and had not turned up any matches in its database.

But, it was clear that the woman had been murdered and someone had murdered her. How the FBI could conclude that there was no connection with the Mardi Gras seemed very shortsighted, particularly in light of the video from the surveillance camera showing someone throwing a black bag overboard from the deck of the Mardi Gras. I was determined to find out who she was and who had murdered her. I hadn't worked homicide for twenty some years for nothing.

58

While I had returned to my old job on the Mardi Gras as head of security, I knew I had to use my time-off to attempt to find the answers to those nagging questions. I had been given access to some information that had not been made public that might help with the investigation. Benson had given me the information even though I had no formal role in the investigation. I think he felt somewhat guilty about how I had been shut out of the original investigation of the Weigand disappearance. One big clue was a tattoo on the torso. On her chest, about midway to the shoulder was a heart tattoo. Inside the heart, the initials "PL" were written in a soft blue color. There was a second set of initials inside the heart below the first set, but those had apparently been erased either deliberately or as a consequence of the decomposition of the body which had taken place. From the photographs I saw, I couldn't tell which it was. Only the very faint outline of one of the letters was visible. To me the letter appeared to be an "R". But Benson and some of the others at the FBI thought it looked more like a "P" or even a "T." Ultimately, Special Agent Benson told me that the FBI lab in Quantico, Virginia had concluded that it could not determine what letter it was.

In any event, the disappearance of Linda Weigand was now being put away in the FBI's archives, along with the case of the victim whose body was found. But I just could not let it go. Images of my missing sister kept flashing through my head. This woman whose body was found, whoever she was, also had a mother, a father, maybe siblings like me and maybe even a husband. Those people had a right to know not only what happened to their loved one, but also who was responsible for her death. I always knew in my heart that there was a person or maybe more than one person who knew what happened to my sister, but no one ever came forward with any information. My mother spent the rest of her life following my sister's disappearance praying that someone, anyone, would come forward with information as to what happened to Teresa when she disappeared while visiting Disneyland. I could not let those people down who were waiting to find out what had happened to their relative or friend. I just could not do so, at least without trying.

59

But, I asked myself, where to start. One thing I could do as a first step was to check the Mardi Gras's passenger list for the cruise when Linda Weigand had disappeared. I was able to bring up the list on my computer in my office and found that there were five persons with the initials. "PL" on board that cruise. Two of the names were those of men, so I quickly dismissed them. But, just to be sure, I called the two and each confirmed that "yes", they were men and were not in fact dead.

That left the three other names with women's names, Pamela Long, Patricia Leyden and Patty Logenfelder. Benson said that they had also checked the passenger list and contacted each of the three women and each told him that "everything is fine, just fine."

I asked Benson if anyone from the FBI had actually gone out to meet with each of the women and he told me that with the budget cutbacks, such travel was "verboten" as he colorfully put it. I still had some of the money that Gorley had given me when I was working for him. I was a little uncomfortable retaining it, but when I asked one of the assistant U.S. attorneys about it, he said to keep the money, "After all, you earned it when you almost got yourself killed." So I decided to keep it and it had tided me over during that period when I was out of work and, seemingly, out of time.

The first woman on the list of persons with the initials PL was Pamela Long. She lived in New

Orleans. I decided I would drive there to see her one Saturday afternoon when the Mardi Gras was in dock in Miami. I had bought a new Honda Civic from Joe Hugo's dealership and he claimed that I got something called "family pricing" on the deal. I didn't know what that meant, but I did know that I still had a monthly car payment to make on a car that I rarely got to use since I was on the ship four months out of every six.

Pamela Long lived in a nice ranch-style house just a few blocks from the annual Mardi Gras parade route. A middle aged woman with light brown hair wearing a pink housedress answered the door after I had rung the bell.

"Ms. Long," I said, "My name is Mario Morales and I am here investigating a potential murder." As I said this, I pulled out my old LAPD badge with the number 1647 on it. I flashed it quickly in front of Ms. Long in the hopes she would not see the image of the Los Angeles' City Hall on it. The badge was just like the one worn by Sergeant Joe Friday on the Dragnet television series in the 1950s. Things hadn't changed much since then.

Mrs. Long appeared rather startled when I said this to her, but after a brief hesitation, she invited me into her ranch house.

"Would you like a glass of iced tea," Mrs. Long asked.

"Yes, that would be fine," I responded. She then disappeared and when she returned she had two glasses of ice tea with her. She handed me one. The tea was so sweet that I almost spat it out. I never did get used to the Southern sweet tea.

I then explained to her about the disappearance of Linda Weigand on the Mardi Gras and the body that had been found with the tattoo. She obviously was not that woman. I assumed this potential lead was going nowhere fast. I was wrong.

Just out of politeness, I asked her if she had enjoyed her cruise.

She said, "Very much so, but I was concerned about one of the women on the cruise."

"What do you mean," I asked.

"Well, the cruise was very nice and I met another single woman who I became friendly with."

"Yes."

"We hung out together after we had been put together at the same table in the main dining room. We would go to the pool and have a drink or two before dinner. But after the third night of the cruise, she just seemed to disappear. I never saw her after that."

"What do you think happened to her?" I asked.

"Well, I thought maybe she found a man on board and she didn't need me anymore to provide her with company. So I didn't even go to her cabin and I never saw her at dinner again."

"If I may ask," I said, "What was the name of this woman?"

"Patricia Leyden. She said she was from Nevada but was living in Miami for the time being. She said that she had some matter she had to work out with her ex-husband. I'm not sure I know what was going on, but they were having some problems."

Shivers literally went up and down my spine as I heard this. "Did she tell you her ex-husband's name?"

Mrs. Long thought for a moment, then said, "Roger, or Robert, something like that. She never mentioned his last name. I guess I assumed it was Leyden, but I'm not sure."

"Mrs. Long, one last question if you don't mind."

"No, of course not, Lieutenant," she replied as we both finished the tea.

"What did this Patricia Leyden look like?"

"She was quite short, about five feet tall only. And she was a brunette, just like me. Pretty lady."

"And how old was she?"

"Oh, we joked about that. We were both 40 years old and we had the same initials. Ironic isn't it that we would come together on this cruise? If you ever happen to see her, please tell her that 'Pamela from the cruise says Hi."

As I walked to my car, one thought kept going through my head. Robert Weigand's first wife lived in Nevada. Mrs. Long thought the first name of the woman's ex-husband may have been named Robert and the heart on the chest of the victim had what appeared to me at least to be an "R". Is it possible the body found off the coast of Cozumel was the body of Robert Weigand's ex-wife? And if so, how did she end up off the coast of Mexico? Then I recalled that Special Agent Benson said they had talked to Patricia Leyden and she was fine. I thought it all the more important I go to her house and see her in person.

I checked the cruise records when I got back to Miami and saw that Patricia Leyden's address was on 17th street. It was a rather old private home that had been converted into 4 apartments. When I rang the doorbell, a woman answered the door.

"My name is Mario Morales and I'm looking for Patricia Leyden. I understand she lives here."

"Not no more," the woman responded. "I'm the landlady and she ain't been back in about two months. I ain't seen hide nor hair of her. And she owes me a month's rent. She left all her stuff here too. I'm gonna have to sell it to cover the rent."

I took this all in as I knew the disappearance of Linda Weigand had taken place just about two months ago.

"When was the last time you saw her?"

"She was getting ready to go on a cruise somewhere. She told me she would be back in a week or so. That was the last time I saw her."

"Did she say anything else?" I asked.

The old woman thought for a moment and then said, "Yeah, she said she was going to duke it out with her ex-husband on the cruise and that her money problems would all be over. Yeah, almost forgot about that."

I could barely contain myself as I asked her, "Did she say the name of her ex-husband?"

"Yeah, sure. She said his name was Robert Weigand, just like that guy who was arrested and on television a couple of weeks ago. Funny coincidence."

The old lady paused for a moment and then said, "That's not the same guy, is it?"

I responded as calmly as I could even though my heart was pounding like crazy. "It is the same guy. It is him," I finally managed to say. "It's him."

60

A week later, Special Agent Benson had the two Weigands brought into the FBI headquarters in Miami for questioning. He invited me to attend the interrogation. I previously had given Benson the gun that I had found in the Captain Vivaldi's cabin the day of Linda Weigand's disappearance. The FBI lab in Quantico, Virginia was able to confirm that the bullet in the torso found off the beach at Cozumel was fired from that gun. The FBI forensic experts also had been able to confirm that the body parts were those of Patricia Leyden through DNA testing comparing her DNA with that of her sister. Patricia Leyden was lost and now she was found.

Benson decided to question Robert Weigand first. Benson wasted no time in the interrogation. As soon as Robert Weigand was brought into the small, cramped interrogation room, Benson asked him point blank: "Why did you kill your ex-wife? Look, we have your gun that killed her, so don't lie to us and say you didn't do it. " None of the details of the discovery of name of the victim had been disclosed publicly yet. Undoubtedly, Weigand must have thought that the questioning would be about the Chinese drug trafficking. Weigand's expression gave away his complete surprise at this line of questioning.

I fully expected Weigand to deny the whole thing, so I was totally unprepared for what happened next.

"I didn't do it. I swear to God, I didn't do it. It was all Linda's fault. She killed her, not me. She killed Patty. It was strictly her idea. I would have given my ex-wife the money she was looking for from the money the Chinese were giving us, but Linda didn't want to part with anything. She wanted it all for us."

I asked if he knew that his ex-wife would be on the cruise.

"No," he said. "It was a complete surprise. But somehow she had gotten wind of what was going on with the Chinese, I'm not sure how, and on the first day of the cruise, she came up to me after my workout in the gym. It was a shock to say the least. I hadn't seen her in over five years. First thing she said to me was, 'I know all about your little game with the Chinese.' At first I pretended like I didn't know what she was talking about. But she knew all about Gorley and Yao and everything else. She started off right away asking for money to keep quiet. When I got back to the cabin I told Linda about it and she was totally outraged. She suggested that we invite her to our suite. I thought she was just going to try to talk her out of blackmailing us. But I guess Linda had other ideas. As soon as Patty came into our suite, Linda confronted Patty, started swearing at her. The next thing I knew, Linda grabbed my gun from the drawer in my end table and Linda shot Patty at close range. Patty dropped like a stone. I went over to her, but she was already dead."

At this point in his story, Weigand began crying just like he had done in our first interview about the disappearance of his wife.

"Whose idea was it to dump her overboard in a black bag?" Benson asked.

"That was my one involvement. I was the one in the video throwing the black bag overboard. I knew we couldn't keep her body on board, so we managed to steal a black garbage bag from the kitchen. I put her in there along with some towels I had used to clean up the blood from the floor of the suite. Early the next morning, I made sure that the steward cleaned our room first to remove any further traces of blood. I'm sorry, really sorry, but it was Linda who went into a rage. I wish to God I could have stopped her. "

As the interrogation was ending, I had a couple of questions for Weigand:

"How did Linda manage to get out of Hugo's suite without being seen on a security camera or triggering the door's keycard record?"

"It was not easy, but she went out onto the balcony of Hugo's room. Once she was outside, she then shinnied across to the balcony of our stateroom next door. I was waiting for her and pulled her across and into our suite. She had practiced on a climbing wall at the gym for weeks and she actually got pretty good hanging from her fingertips. I almost lost her once, but she made it across."

"I take it that Linda then stayed in Patty Leyden's cabin and posed as her when leaving the ship?" I asked.

"Yeah, it was kinda weird. Linda bought some hair dye in the ship's gift shop and dyed her hair to match Patty's. When I saw her with the dyed hair, I was surprised how much she actually looked like Patty. I had never noticed that before."

61

Three weeks later, based on his confession, Robert was charged with being an accessory after the fact to the murder of Patricia Leyden. He pleaded guilty several months later and received a sentence of five to seven years in prison. Linda refused a plea bargain and went to trial before Judge McFarland. The jury found her guilty of murder in the second degree and she received a life sentence. She will be eligible for parole in thirty years.

Because Yao Lin had returned to China under the protection of diplomatic immunity, Sun Li was the only person from the Chinese side who could be prosecuted. Because of her cooperation with the federal prosecutor, she was given only a year in prison and two years' probation for her part in the plot. I visited her once while she was in prison and I think that when she is released I may give her a call. Yeah, I think I will do that.

One last item had to be tied up in my mind and that was how Patricia Leyden knew about the Chinese plot to acquire the Mariner cruise line and the Weigands' involvement in that plot. I'm afraid she took that information to the grave. But I was glad to help bring some closure to this case and to Patricia Leyden's family. In the end, it is ironic that a partially erased tattoo was the Weigands' undoing. It was as though Patricia Leyden was somehow able to bring about her own closure.

The End

Made in the USA
Charleston, SC
14 November 2016